THE ZOMBIE
by
MORTON CARVER

Dedicated to James Carver Sr., for humoring a 19 year old writer who thought he was Stephen King all those years ago, and for showing him exactly why he wasn't.
Most of all, for treasuring this story in your safe for two decades in an envelope marked simply *'Mort's bestseller'*. - MC

JULY 17, YEAR UNKNOWN

The world's no longer what it used to be. The hustle and bustle of human life, the chaos of their existence... all of it has been replaced by a deafening silence and desolation that's haunting in its purity. I am alone. I have been alone for too long.
Humans. They've reclaimed their cities, their world. They're the survivors, the victorious species. And I? I am their enemy, their nightmare, a hideous remnant of a time they'd rather forget.
They call me a monster, a mindless beast, but that's not true. I can think. I can feel. Pain. Hunger. Loneliness. I am not what they made us out to be. I am a zombie, yes. But I am also the last. The last zombie.

Today, I wandered through the ruins of what was once a great city. A city filled with life and laughter, now a skeletal reminder of what used to be. The torn posters, the abandoned toys, the crumbling buildings... they all tell a tale. A tale of survival. A tale of loss.
I'm keeping this diary - an irony, I know. A zombie's diary. But then again, I'm no ordinary zombie. I'm the last. I need to remember, I need to document, I need to find others, if there are any left.
My search was fruitless today, as it has been for the past countless days. Every corner I turn, every alley I traverse, it's the same. Emptiness. Silence.
But I'm not giving up. There must be others. I can't be the only one left. I won't accept that.
I may be a monster in the eyes of the humans, but to me, they are the real monsters. They hunted us, cornered us, wiped us out. Now, they're hunting me.
There's a part of me, a human part, that fears them. Fears extinction. Fears the end. But there's another part, a newer, fiercer part that's determined. Determined to survive. To persist.
Tomorrow, I'll search again. I'll wander through the remains of the world that once was, seeking signs of my kind.
I am the last zombie. And this is my diary. This is my story. My fight for survival. My fight for existence.

JULY 18, YEAR UNKNOWN

Today, the sky cried. The rain, once an inconvenience to the living, felt strangely comforting, like the world sharing in my solitude. It washed the city, the remnants of the old world, almost as if trying to cleanse it of its sins.
I spent most of the day under the crumbling arch of what once was a grand library. Its once majestic columns now scarred and weathered. Shelves upon shelves of wisdom, soaked and wasted. In this new world, survival outranked wisdom, it seemed.

But amidst the ruins, I found something. A book, untouched by the rain. It was a collection of tales from different cultures about the end of the world. Ironic. But I felt drawn to it. To the tales of apocalypse, of survival, of hope.
Despite the hunger, the constant ache, I spent the day reading. The stories varied wildly yet had the same theme: the end is not really the end. There's always something that survives, something that persists. I found a strange kind of comfort in that.

Towards dusk, I heard it. A distant sound, almost like a growl. My heart raced, a sensation I hadn't felt in what seemed like a lifetime. I wanted to believe it was one of my own. I wanted to believe I was not alone.
In the dimming light, I followed the sound, stumbling through the wet, empty streets. I hoped against all odds to see the twisted form of another like me in the encroaching darkness.
But when I reached the source, my heart sank. It was just a lone dog, ribs showing, foraging for food in a pile of garbage. The disappointment was bitter, a pill hard to swallow. I was still alone.

But then, something happened. The dog, it didn't run away from me. It growled, barked, then sat, looking at me with eyes as lost as mine. For a moment, we shared something. A silent acknowledgment of our shared loneliness, our shared struggle.

Tonight, I write this entry with the dog curled up beside me. It's no zombie, but it's a form of companionship I hadn't thought I'd experience again. It's strange and comforting.

Today wasn't the day I found my kind, but it wasn't a complete loss either. I found a friend in a world that's forgotten the meaning of the word.
Tomorrow, the search continues. But for tonight, I'll take comfort in this small victory.

I am the last zombie. But tonight, I'm a little less alone.

JULY 19, YEAR UNKNOWN

Today, I named the dog. "Rain". It seemed fitting. In this grim world of emptiness, she's a spark of something I had forgotten. A reminder of a time before, a time where I might have patted a dog, laughed at their antics. It's a hollow memory, like an echo fading into the distance, but it's mine nonetheless.

Rain stayed by my side as we wandered the streets, a steady presence by my side. She whined when she got too hungry, and I had to scrounge around to find something edible for her. The sight of her eating was both painful and comforting. I know what hunger feels like, but not the satisfaction of quelling it.

There's no sign of my kind. Every corner, every turn, every hushed whisper of the wind feels like a cruel joke now. But I press on. Rain, in her own way, gives me strength. I can't tell if she understands, but when my steps falter, she nudges me, pushing me to keep moving.
The city is becoming more hostile. I can sense the humans closing in. Gunshots in the distance, the drone of helicopters overhead. They're hunting. I'm the prey.

I found a place to hide today - an old, abandoned subway station. It's dark, it's damp, but it's safe. For now. Rain seems restless, her keen ears catching sounds that I'm not capable of hearing anymore. I pat her, trying to give her a sense of calm. It's strange, this act of comfort. I don't know who it soothes more - her or me.

Tonight, I feel a chill that doesn't stem from the cold of the subway. It's a premonition, a sense of impending danger. I'm not sure how long I can avoid the humans, how long I can keep up this search.

But as I pen down this entry, Rain's warm body curled up against me, I know I can't give up. Not yet. I owe it to myself. To her. To the world that might have been. I am the last. But as long as I'm here, we're not completely gone.

Tomorrow, the hunt continues. For my kind. For safety. For survival.

I am the last zombie. I carry the weight of extinction, but also the hope of persistence.

JULY 20, YEAR UNKNOWN

It was today I realized that Rain is not just a companion, but a protector. The morning was a gray wash, a perfect mirror to my mood. The drones from yesterday had grown louder, closer. But Rain... she seemed to sense the danger before it arrived.

As the drone of helicopters became an ominous growl, she began to growl too, a low threatening sound that filled the underground space. She was alert, ears pricked, eyes fixed on the entrance of our hideaway.

Then they came, a swarm of humans dressed in military green. Guns pointed, ready to wipe out what they perceived as a threat. I was ready to meet my end but Rain had other plans.

She leapt out of the shadows, a blur of desperation and fangs. The humans were taken aback. They hadn't expected a dog, a "pet." But Rain was no ordinary pet. She was a survivor, just like me. Her distraction provided the precious moments I needed to escape through the back tunnels of the subway.

The guilt of leaving her behind stings like a fresh wound. But I know she did what she did for survival. Not just hers, but mine too. I hope, with all the semblance of a heart I have left, that she made it out.

In the dim light of the tunnels, I penned this entry. The lack of Rain's warmth is a painful reminder of the price of survival. Her bravery, her sacrifice, will not be forgotten. Today, she saved the last zombie, she gave me another chance to search, to survive.

Tomorrow, I plan to find her, to return to her what she gave me - a fighting chance. But for tonight, I mourn her absence.

I am the last zombie. I continue to exist, to persist, carrying the memory of a dog named Rain.

JULY 21, YEAR UNKNOWN

My search for Rain began with the dawn. I retraced my steps, prowling around our last sanctuary, but it was swarming with humans. I could not risk it. I ventured out into the periphery, hoping against hope. By nightfall, there was no sign of her. I felt her absence more acutely than ever.

JULY 22, YEAR UNKNOWN

Today, I found a sliver of hope. A paw print in the mud, a familiar whine carried by the wind. She was close. I followed the signs, my undead heart pounding with anticipation. But as night fell, I found nothing. I hold on to the fading thread of her memory. It's all I've got.

JULY 23, YEAR UNKNOWN

Today, I caught a whiff of something. It was faint, but it was there. The scent of fur, of dog, of Rain. I pursued it with everything I had. It led me to an abandoned warehouse on the outskirts of the city. As I ventured inside, I found a nest, a remnant of warmth. But no Rain. I camped there for the night, praying for a miracle.

JULY 24, YEAR UNKNOWN

The miracle happened. I woke up to the lick of a warm tongue, the thump of a wagging tail. It was Rain. She was thinner, a scar running down her side, but it was her. Our reunion was quiet, no celebrations, no grand gestures. Just the simple comfort of companionship regained. Tonight, I feel a strange emotion. Relief, I think. Or joy. Maybe both.

JULY 25, YEAR UNKNOWN

Today was a day of rest. A day to let Rain heal, to let us heal. We foraged for food, found a small stream nearby. Life was simple. It felt good. It felt... right. The search for my kind can wait. For now, survival and companionship are enough.

JULY 26, YEAR UNKNOWN

The peace was shattered by the distant drone of helicopters. They were still searching, still hunting. We had to move. With Rain by my side, we ventured deeper into the outskirts, leaving the city behind. Tonight, we rest under the open sky. The stars seem brighter, more hopeful.

JULY 27, YEAR UNKNOWN

Today, we encountered another living being. A deer. It looked at us, its eyes wide with fear, then bolted. It's been a long time since I saw another creature that was not a threat. It felt strangely comforting, this reminder that life persists, in one form or another. Tonight, as I write this down, my gnarled hand trembles. I am filled with a newfound determination.

I am the last zombie. With Rain by my side, I continue my quest, fighting not just for survival, but for life in all its forms.

JULY 28, YEAR UNKNOWN

Our journey away from the city continues. Today, we trekked through dense forests, overgrown with years of neglect. Rain seemed to thrive in this environment, her instincts guiding us through the tangle of foliage.

As the sun set, we stumbled upon an old cabin, hidden deep within the forest. Abandoned but sturdy, it promised a much-needed respite from our journey. Inside, there were remnants of a life once lived - a faded family picture, a child's toy, a fireplace that once roared with warmth.

I made it as comfortable as I could for Rain. Her wound from the city encounter seems to be healing well, but she needs rest. As for me, I find comfort in the silence of the woods, a stark contrast to the concrete desolation of the city.

Tonight, I ponder on the world that was and the world that is. It's strange how nature has reclaimed what was once hers, erasing traces of human existence. It's a silent reminder of our impermanence, of the fleeting nature of power and control.

Tomorrow, we continue. But for tonight, in the heart of the wilderness, within the walls of this cabin, we find peace.

I am the last zombie. In the solitude of the wilderness, accompanied by Rain, I continue to seek, to survive, to persist.

JULY 29, YEAR UNKNOWN

We spent the day exploring the surroundings of the cabin. Deep in the woods, the sounds of nature created a melody unlike any I've heard since the world turned upside down. Birds chirping, the rustle of leaves underfoot, the distant rush of a river, all of it soothing, grounding.

In the evening, I found something surprising in the dense foliage - a garden, overgrown but still bearing fruits. Apple trees, laden with fruits of survival. Their sweet smell reminded me of a time when I could taste, when I could relish such simple joys. I picked some for Rain. Watching her eat was a bittersweet joy.

Tonight, I pen this down with a sense of tranquility I haven't felt in a long time. The woods are silent, save for the nocturnal chorus of crickets. For a moment, I can almost forget what I am, what we're up against.

JULY 30, YEAR UNKNOWN

Today, we stayed close to the cabin. Rain, adventurous as ever, found a small pond teeming with fish. She splashed around, her playful antics a reminder of the world that was. I watched her, an undead spectator to a spectacle of life.

The simplicity of today felt like a balm to the wounds of our journey. But the peace here is a double-edged sword. It's comforting, yes, but also a stark reminder of my solitude, of my uniqueness in this post-apocalyptic world.

As night falls, I can't help but ponder - is it worth continuing the search? Is there a point in seeking what may not exist? But then I look at Rain, her body curled up near the crackling fireplace, and I know I can't give up. Not yet.

JULY 31, YEAR UNKNOWN

Our peaceful existence was interrupted today. The distant drone of a helicopter, a ghost from the past, sent us into high alert. But the vastness of the forest and the hidden location of the cabin worked in our favor. The human world buzzed over us, unaware of our existence below.

Despite the scare, life in the cabin resumed its normal pace. But I'm aware that we're on borrowed time. This sanctuary, this slice of peace, is temporary. One day, we'll have to move, venture back into the unknown.

As I write this entry, I feel a mix of resignation and determination. The journey is hard, the destination unknown, yet I press on. Because the alternative is to surrender, to give up, and I am not ready for that.

I am the last zombie. With Rain, I walk the line between a haunting past and an uncertain future, carrying the weight of an extinct species.

AUGUST 1, YEAR UNKNOWN

Today was a day of exploration. We ventured further into the woods, drawn by the peaceful rhythm of nature around us. Rain led the way, her senses honed by instinct and survival. The quiet serenity was punctuated only by the occasional rustling of leaves or a bird's call.

In the afternoon, we came across another deer. It stopped in its tracks, looking at us with wide, curious eyes. The moment stretched out, a tableau of the unexpected. Then, as swiftly as it had appeared, the deer bounded away, disappearing into the dense foliage. As I watched it go, I felt a strange connection to this creature. Both of us were survivors, creatures adrift in a world that was simultaneously ours and not.

At night, nestled in the cabin, the day's encounter weighed heavily on my mind. Even as the last of my kind, I was part of this grand cycle of life and death. A cog in the wheel, turning endlessly. The thought was humbling.

AUGUST 2, YEAR UNKNOWN

The day brought an unexpected discovery. In a dusty corner of the cabin, I found an old journal. Its pages were yellowed with age, filled with neat handwriting that spoke of past lives and forgotten dreams.

Reading through them, I was struck by a profound sense of connection. Here was a glimpse into a world that was long gone, into lives that were lived fully and then extinguished. It was an echo of my own past life as a human, of days filled with joy, sadness, hope, and despair.

The more I read, the more I felt a strange kinship with the journal's owner. Their joys, their sorrows, their dreams, their fears, all resonated with me. It was a poignant reminder of the transient nature of life, of the fleeting moments that make up our existence.

AUGUST 3, YEAR UNKNOWN

Today was a day of survival. With Rain by my side, we spent the better part of the day foraging. The forest, once intimidating in its wildness, was now our provider. It was a humbling experience, this reliance on nature for sustenance.

By evening, we were laden with fruits, nuts, and berries. It was a strange sight, I suppose, a zombie and a dog, living off the land. But it was our reality, our world. Back in the cabin, I prepared a meal for Rain, watching as she devoured the food with a fervor that was both endearing and heartbreaking. I was reminded, yet again, of the cost of survival.

Tonight, by the warmth of the fire, Rain sleeping peacefully by my side, I take a moment to reflect on our journey. The solitude, the danger, the constant threat of discovery, it all seems worth it for these moments of peace. It's a dangerous world out there, but for now, we're safe.

We're survivors. Rain and I. And as the last zombie, I'm determined to keep it that way.

AUGUST 4, YEAR UNKNOWN

Today's exploration led us off the beaten path. Rain and I stumbled upon something remarkable hidden within the heart of the forest - an old, forgotten theater. Its grand facade, though now weathered and overgrown, still held hints of its former glory. Flickering lights still twinkled through broken window frames. A solar cell laden roof lay half buried in moss and decay. An unexpected monument in the midst of the wilderness, it intrigued me.

Nature had made its claim, weaving a tapestry of vines over the stone and wood. The entrance was shrouded in undergrowth, the doors barely visible. But it was the promise of what lay within those heavy doors that piqued my curiosity.

The setting sun cast long shadows over the forest, adding an eerie beauty to the scene. As I looked at the theater, the strange building in this unlikely place, my mind filled with possibilities. Could it hold answers, or maybe even a connection to the past? Was it a relic best left undisturbed, or a path leading to an unknown adventure?

Tonight, as I write this entry in the soft glow of our campfire, the image of the theater looms in my mind. The questions remain unanswered, the doors unopened. Yet, there is a sense of anticipation in the air. Rain, in her canine wisdom, seems to sense it too, her gaze often turning towards the hidden building as she lays by my side.

I am the last zombie. Tomorrow holds the promise of a new discovery, a new path in our journey. As the last embers of the fire flicker out, I feel a strange sense of excitement. The theater waits, silent and enigmatic, as we prepare to unveil its mask.

AUGUST 5, YEAR UNKNOWN

Dawn broke, casting a golden light over the wilderness as we made our way back to the theater. The building seemed more formidable in the daylight, its timeworn grandeur amplified by the morning sun. Today was the day we would uncover its secrets.

Our approach, however, was thwarted by an unexpected obstacle. The main entrance, the grand doors hidden beneath the undergrowth, was sealed off by a landslide. A mound of earth and stone blocked our path, a testament to the relentless march of time.

For a moment, disappointment clouded my thoughts. But then, Rain, ever the embodiment of her namesake, perked up her ears and wagged her tail. I was reminded that every problem, every obstacle, held the potential for a solution.

And so, we set off again, this time with a new goal. Our journey led us further into the wilderness, in search of tools that could aid us. Old camping sites, abandoned cabins, wreckage from the past – we combed through them all, driven by a sense of purpose.

By dusk, we *(I include Rain out of politeness, she did very little to help)* had collected an assortment of rudimentary tools – a couple of sturdy branches, a metal rod, and a hand shovel weathered by time. It wasn't much, but it was a start. As night fell, we returned to our makeshift home, weary yet hopeful.

I am the last zombie, and tonight, I find myself staring at the tools we've gathered, my mind filled with plans and possibilities. The theater, with its tantalizing promise, waits for us. And tomorrow, we shall take the first step in unveiling its secrets.

AUGUST 6, YEAR UNKNOWN

As morning broke, Rain and I found ourselves back at the base of the landslide, our collected tools spread out before us. In the soft light of the rising sun, we began our work. Each tool was inspected carefully, each potential use evaluated. A simple metal rod, weathered and rusted by the elements, held potential as a pry bar. Sturdy branches could act as levers, providing the much-needed force to move larger boulders. The hand shovel, though aged and worn, was sturdy enough to shift the smaller debris. Rain watched in attentive silence as I arranged and rearranged our implements, my brain meticulously planning our day's work.

And so, we spent the morning. The world around us was alive with the sounds of the wilderness. The chirping of far-off birds, the rustling of leaves in the soft wind, the distant murmur of a stream – they formed a strange symphony, a stark contrast to the silence of our solitude.

By midday, we had made significant progress. The mound of earth and stones had started to yield under our relentless efforts. A corner of the grand doors was now visible, the once bright paint peeling and faded but hinting at its past grandeur. Seeing our progress sparked a glimmer of anticipation within me - soon, we'd be able to enter the theater.

As the sun began to set, painting the sky with hues of orange and pink, we retreated to our camp for the day. As I sat by our makeshift fire, staring at the flickering flames, my thoughts turned to the theater. What would we find inside? Would there be a clue to our salvation, a beacon of hope in our desolate existence? Or would it just be another monument to a world long lost?

AUGUST 7, YEAR UNKNOWN

Another day, another step closer to our goal. The rhythm of our existence now revolved around our mission – wake up at dawn, work on the landslide, take breaks to scavenge for food and supplies, and retreat to our camp when darkness started to creep in. Every shovelful of earth moved, every stone displaced, brought us closer to the secrets hidden behind the theater's grand doors.

But the physical labor wasn't the only thing occupying my thoughts. More and more, I found myself remembering snippets of my past life. The sound of laughter echoing in a packed hall, the hum of conversation around a dinner table, the sweet notes of a piano playing a familiar melody. The world used to be filled with these sounds, with life and vibrancy. But now, the silence was almost deafening.

AUGUST 8, YEAR UNKNOWN

My dreams have become a strange mirror to my waking hours. They're filled with visions of the past, of the world as it used to be. Crowded streets bustling with life, parks filled with children's laughter, cafes resonating with the murmur of conversations. But every morning, I'd wake up to a world that was a stark contrast to my dreams. The silence, the emptiness, they're constant reminders of our isolation.

And yet, amidst all the reminders of what used to be, there was an undercurrent of anticipation, of hope. Each day brought us closer to our goal. Each day was a step towards potential salvation. Perhaps the theater, with its promise of untold secrets, would hold the key to our deliverance.

AUGUST 9, YEAR UNKNOWN

Today marked a significant milestone in our journey. After what feels like weeks of unyielding labor, the grand doors of the theater were finally revealed in their entirety. Their design, though marred by time and neglect, spoke volumes of their past magnificence. I stood before them, a sense of achievement washing over me. Our mission was far from over, but this was a start.

As night fell, I found myself back at the campfire, the flickering flames casting long shadows. The theater's entrance, looming in the distance, seemed to beckon us, urging us to uncover its secrets. Tomorrow, we would step into the unknown, moving closer to the answers we sought. As I pen down these thoughts in my diary, the only record of our journey, I couldn't help but feel that our lives were about to change significantly. Whatever lay on the other side of those doors, it held the promise of a future, of a possibility that perhaps, just perhaps, we were not alone in this world.

AUGUST 10, YEAR UNKNOWN

The morning came with a sense of anticipation that hung in the air, almost tangible. Today was the day. We stood before the grand doors, their age and neglect only adding to their gravitas. With a deep breath, I pushed against the heavy wood, the doors creaking open to reveal the world that lay within.

The interior of the theater was a time capsule, a slice of the world preserved from before the fall. Dust hung heavy in the air, disturbed by our entrance. Rows of velvet-covered seats, faded with time, stretched out before a grand stage, the curtain drawn. The silence was almost deafening. It was a monument to a time of stories and dreams, a stark contrast to the harsh reality of our existence.

AUGUST 11, YEAR UNKNOWN

We spent the day exploring the theater. The auditorium led to a network of hallways, each one revealing a new aspect of the theater. Dressing rooms with mirrors still intact, costumes still hanging on racks, a room filled with reels of films, each one meticulously labeled. The ghosts of stories untold, of dreams unfulfilled, seemed to permeate the air.

Despite the eeriness, there was an odd comfort in these relics of the past. They were reminders of a time when stories mattered, when dreams were shared, when life was more than mere survival.

AUGUST 12, YEAR UNKNOWN

In a forgotten corner of the theater, I found an old film projector. Covered in a thick layer of dust, it was a relic of a time long past. As I cleaned it off and examined the machine, a thought crossed my mind. Would it still work? Could the old reels of film still tell their stories?

AUGUST 13, YEAR UNKNOWN

With a bit of tinkering, a lot of guesswork, and a little bit of luck, I managed to get the old projector to work. The light flickered to life, casting an uneven glow on the grand screen. Rain seemed as surprised as me, her head tilting in curiosity at the play of light and shadow.

AUGUST 14, YEAR UNKNOWN

Our first film night. I picked a reel at random, the label long since faded. The whirring of the projector filled the theater, a comforting sound in the silence. The screen came alive with moving pictures, a black-and-white world playing out before our eyes. A silent film, a drama, from the looks of it. I found myself drawn in, the simplistic storytelling a soothing balm for my weary soul.

AUGUST 15, YEAR UNKNOWN

We've settled into a routine, a semblance of normality amidst our extraordinary circumstances. Our days are spent exploring the theater and its many secrets, our nights lost in the stories the old films tell. Each reel brings a new adventure, a new tale to get lost in. Amidst the harsh reality of our existence, they provide a moment of respite, a moment of escape into a world that once was.

AUGUST 16, YEAR UNKNOWN

There is an inexplicable connection between this theater and myself now. It's as though it has stories to share, and I'm the only audience it has left. Each corner, each hidden room whispers tales of the past. The laughter and applause, the gasps of surprise, the silent tears - all echoes of the emotions that once filled this place. Now, it's just Rain and me, listening to the silence and the stories it tells.

AUGUST 17, YEAR UNKNOWN

Our days pass in this cycle of discovery and exploration. The theater holds an array of rooms – dressing rooms with long-forgotten costumes, projection rooms filled with dust-covered reels, an orchestra pit that hasn't seen a performance in an eternity. Each holds a piece of a past that seems increasingly alien to me, yet oddly comforting.

AUGUST 18, YEAR UNKNOWN

An unexpected find today. Tucked away in a hidden compartment of the projection room, I found a collection of documentaries. They were older, judging by the packaging, possibly recorded before the outbreak. Could they hold any clue about the world before all of this happened?

AUGUST 19, YEAR UNKNOWN

I stayed up late into the night watching the documentaries. They were a stark reminder of the world that was - vibrant, thriving, and undeniably human. It was a world that I remembered, but from a distance, as if through a veil. These films, they were like windows into a past that seems both familiar and strange.

AUGUST 20, YEAR UNKNOWN

One documentary, in particular, caught my attention. It was about a group of scientists who were working on advanced medical treatments. It was eerie watching their hopeful faces, listening to their enthusiastic voices, knowing what the future held. But there was one detail that made me sit up - their research facility.

AUGUST 21, YEAR UNKNOWN

I must have watched that section of the film a hundred times. There, hidden in plain sight, was the location of the facility. I knew those mountains. I had walked that way many years ago. If there was a chance that any of those treatments had survived, if there was a hope that something could reverse this curse of un-death, it would be there. I felt my mind shift. Like a cog ratcheting purposefully onto the next tooth. No longer was finding others like me the driving force. There was suddenly a chance to help them all. To help me. To rid myself of this curse.

AUGUST 22, YEAR UNKNOWN

As dawn broke, I found myself filled with a renewed sense of purpose. For the first time in a long while, there was a glimmer of hope, a possible path leading towards a solution. I knew what our next destination would be - the research facility. The theater had given us much, but it was time to move on. Tomorrow, we set off on a new journey.

AUGUST 23, YEAR UNKNOWN

The day was a flurry of activity. We had to prepare for our journey, gather our supplies, ensure we had everything we would need. The theater had been a place of solace, of reprieve, but it was time to move on. I found myself walking its hallways, through the auditorium, tracing my fingers along the peeling wallpaper and worn-out seats. It was like saying goodbye to an old friend.

The theater had been more than just a shelter. It was a reminder of the world that was, of humanity's triumphs and failures, of our capacity to dream and create. It had given us a purpose, a direction, and now, it was pointing us towards our next adventure.

As I packed our belongings, I couldn't help but glance at the rows upon rows of film reels. These silent witnesses to a forgotten era held stories untold, dreams unfulfilled. They were a slice of the past, a testament to our ability to hope and imagine.

In the midst of packing, I noticed something unusual - a reel of film that didn't match the rest. It was newer, its label still intact. Intrigued, I set aside the packing and set up the projector. The film came alive, casting shadows and light across the auditorium.

To my surprise, the film was not a feature film or documentary, but what seemed to be a series of news reports. The date stamp in the corner indicated they were from just before the outbreak. It was a surreal experience, watching the world fall into chaos through the lens of a news camera. The escalating reports, the growing fear, the eventual collapse - it was all there, recorded in black and white.

I sat there long after the reel had ended, the image of the world unraveling before my eyes etched into my memory. As haunting as it was, it also served as a reminder of why we were doing this - why we were embarking on this journey.

As I retired for the night, my mind was filled with images from the past and plans for the future. Tomorrow, we would step into the unknown, carrying the weight of our past and the hope of a future.

AUGUST 24, YEAR UNKNOWN

We set off at dawn. The theater stood tall against the rising sun, its faded grandeur a stark contrast to the wilderness around it. As we moved further away, I found myself glancing back, the silhouette of the theater growing smaller with each passing moment. It felt strange, leaving behind the place that had been our home, our sanctuary. But ahead lay a path filled with promise, a beacon of hope in our desolate existence.

The journey was uneventful, our path taking us through a landscape filled with remnants of a world long lost. Abandoned buildings, overgrown parks, empty roads - each held a story, a memory of the life that once thrived there. Despite the emptiness, there was a sense of life still persisting, nature reclaiming what once was its own.

As night fell, we made camp by the roadside. The night was calm, a blanket of stars stretching across the sky. The quiet was broken only by the occasional hoot of an owl or the rustling of leaves in the wind. In the silence, my thoughts turned to our mission, to the path ahead. We were charting a course into the unknown, guided only by the sliver of hope the theater had gifted us.

As I settled down for the night, I felt a strange sense of peace. The journey ahead was filled with uncertainty, but there was also hope - a light guiding us through the darkness. Perhaps, just perhaps, we were on the path to salvation.

AUGUST 25, YEAR UNKNOWN

We continued our journey at first light. The path was arduous, with nature's reclaiming touch making progress slow. But we trudged on, the promise of what lay ahead driving us forward. As we navigated the overgrown roads and through dilapidated buildings, I couldn't help but marvel at nature's resilience. Despite the desolation, life found a way to endure, to flourish.

As the sun dipped below the horizon, we found an abandoned farmhouse to take shelter for the night. It was in surprisingly good condition, with the main structure still intact. It was a welcome respite after the long day of travel. As we settled in for the night, the thoughts of the journey ahead filled my mind.

Each day brought us closer to our goal, to the hope of finding answers, of finding a way to reverse this limbo of undeath. I found my thoughts drifting back to the theater, to the stories it held, to the hope it had given us. As I drifted off to sleep, I found myself hoping that our journey would lead to a happy ending, just like the stories from the old films.

AUGUST 26, YEAR UNKNOWN

As we resumed our journey, the reality of our mission became more tangible. With each passing day, the possibility of finding answers, of finding a cure, became more real. The world around us seemed to echo our hopes, with the sun shining brighter, the wind carrying whispers of encouragement.

We made good progress today, the terrain growing more familiar, more reminiscent of the world as it once was. As we ventured deeper into the heartland, we started encountering more signs of human activity, frozen in time - fences, roads, even a deserted vehicle or two. They served as a reminder of the world we had lost, of the lives that once thrived here. Yet, they also served as a beacon, a sign that we were on the right path.

As night fell, we found shelter in an old outhouse. Its sturdy walls provided a much-needed barrier from the harsh winds. As I settled in for the night, my thoughts were an onslaught of possibilities, of hopes and fears. We were closer than ever to our destination, to the answers we sought. With each passing day, the dream of a future, of an end to this nightmare, seemed more attainable.

We had faced numerous challenges on our journey, each one testing our resolve, our will to carry on. But with each obstacle, we had emerged stronger, more determined. As I closed my eyes, I felt a sense of anticipation, a sense of promise. Tomorrow held the promise of a new beginning, of a step closer to our goal.

As the last vestiges of consciousness slipped away, I found myself filled with a renewed sense of purpose. We were on the right path, the path toward hope. And with each passing day, we were moving closer to our goal, to the end of this nightmare.

AUGUST 27, YEAR UNKNOWN

The reflection in the cracked mirror startled me today. The figure staring back was a shell of the man I once was - a pallid, gaunt figure with lifeless eyes. My skin, stretched taut over a skeletal frame, carried the pallor of death. The sight was a grim reminder of my undead existence, of the horrifying reality that was me.

The mirror bumped and shattered as I involuntarily recoiled. The shards fell like crystallized tears, their sharp edges catching the morning light. Each piece held a distorted image, a grotesque caricature of my existence. I stood there weeping, my reflection fragmented, mirroring the shattered remnants of my humanity.

Rain, my constant companion, seemed to sense my distress. As I turned towards her, I saw a flicker of fear in her eyes for the first time. The realization stung more than any physical pain. She was afraid, afraid of me. I saw her take a step back, her body tensed, ready to flee.

I had always taken comfort in the fact that despite all, she never viewed me with fear. She had been my tether to the world, a reminder of the love and loyalty that defined humanity. But now, seeing fear in her eyes, it felt as if that tether was slipping away.

I spent the day in silence, lost in my thoughts. The incident had stirred up feelings I had buried deep within - despair, loneliness, and a sense of loss. I was reminded of the world I was cut off from, the human emotions and connections I could no longer be a part of.

As the day gave way to night, I found myself grappling with a torrent of emotions. The bleak reminder of my undead existence had cast a shadow over our journey. The hope of finding a cure, of regaining my humanity, felt like a distant dream.

But I also knew that I couldn't afford to lose hope. For Rain's sake, for my own, I had to keep moving forward. The fear in

Rain's eyes had subsided by evening, replaced by her familiar warmth. But the image was etched in my mind, a reminder of the line that separated us.

Tomorrow, we would resume our journey. But today, today was tainted by the cost of this curse, of the isolating chasm between my undead existence and the vibrant world of the living. As I finally drifted off to sleep, I couldn't shake off the image in the mirror - the image of the last zombie.

AUGUST 28, YEAR UNKNOWN

I woke to the soft light of dawn filtering through the cracks in the walls. Rain was curled up next to me, her warm body a comforting presence. Seeing her there, peaceful and trusting, reassured me. Our bond was stronger than the fears of yesterday.

We set out early, the weight of yesterday's encounter heavy in my mind. The journey was quiet, each of us lost in our thoughts. The world around us unfolded in varying shades of gray and green, the ruins of humanity juxtaposed with the relentless advance of nature. The sight was both depressing and inspiring - a stark mirror of our failure, and yet a testament to life's enduring resilience.

As we traversed through the abandoned towns and overgrown highways, I noticed the silent witnesses to the world that once was - vacant homes, discarded belongings, cars left to rust. These artifacts of the past told tales of loss and desolation, of a world brought to its knees by a devastating plague.

Yet, within this desolation, there was hope. Nature was reclaiming its rightful place, thriving in the ruins of humanity. Trees sprouted from cracked pavements, flowers bloomed from the rubble, and wildlife roamed free in the abandoned towns. It was a sobering reminder that life goes on, adapting and evolving, no matter the circumstances.

As night fell, we found shelter in the remnants of a library. Its decaying shelves held the wisdom and imagination of a bygone era - books of every genre, covering every conceivable topic. These vestiges of human intellect and creativity stood as a testament to our capacity to dream, to aspire, to grow. They were symbols of hope among the despair, a beacon of light in the darkness.

I picked a book at random and settled down for the night. Reading by the dim light, I felt a strange sense of connection - a link to the world that was, to the dreams and hopes of a different time. Despite everything, the spark of humanity still survived - in the loyalty of a dog, in the endurance of nature, in the silent pages of a book.

Today was a reminder of the duality of my existence - of the despair that came with the knowledge of my poisoned state, and the hope that spurred me on. But for now, I took solace in the simple act of reading, of connecting with the humanity I longed to regain. The journey would continue tomorrow, bringing us a day closer to our goal, to our salvation. But for tonight, I found comfort in the world of words, in the whispers of the past.

AUGUST 29, YEAR UNKNOWN

The morning came with the promise of a new day. We resumed our journey, our path lit by the warm rays of the rising sun. The day passed uneventfully, the landscape unfolding in an endless stretch of green and gray.

Our progress was slow, the overgrown vegetation and debris making navigation difficult. But we trudged on, driven by the hope of reaching our destination. Despite the hardships, there was a strange sense of peace, a rhythm to our journey. The world around us might have been a post-apocalyptic wasteland, but it was our world, and we had learned to adapt, to survive.

By mid-afternoon, we reached the outskirts of what seemed to be a large city. Its tall structures stood as silent sentinels, a stark reminder of the bustling life that once thrived here. The sight was a mix of awe and sadness - awe at the achievements of humanity, and sadness at its downfall.

We decided to camp at the edge of the city, taking shelter in an old bus station. As I sat watching the sun set, painting the cityscape in warm hues, I couldn't help but wonder about the stories these structures held. Lives lived, dreams dreamt, hopes nurtured - all silenced by the devastating plague.

As night fell, the city transformed into an eerie landscape, its darkened structures looming like ominous shadows. The silence was broken only by the howl of the wind, the rustle of leaves, and the occasional distant howl of a lone wolf. Despite the desolation, there was a strange beauty to it, a serenity that belied the devastation.

As I settled in for the night, I found my thoughts drifting to our goal, to the promise of a cure. The journey was arduous, the challenges numerous. But with each passing day, we were getting closer, inching towards the possibility of salvation. The thought was a beacon in the darkness, a glimmer of hope amidst the despair. As I drifted off to sleep, I was filled with a sense of anticipation. The city held many mysteries, many stories. But for us, it was another step in our journey, another step towards our goal.

And so, with the city as our next challenge, we continued on our path - the path of hope, of redemption, of survival. I am the last zombie, and this is our journey.

AUGUST 30, YEAR UNKNOWN

As dawn broke, we set off towards the city, its skeletal structures casting long shadows in the morning light. The closer we got, the more tangible the reminders of humanity's downfall became. Empty cars lined the streets, shop windows were shattered, and every surface seemed to be decorated by the slow encroachment of vines and moss. It felt like stepping into a graveyard, an echoing silence that was both profound and unsettling.

In this silence, I was reminded of my solitary existence. I was a creature of death walking through the remnants of life, an outsider looking in. And yet, there was an odd sense of familiarity, a vague recollection of a life that once was. The deserted cityscape was a stark contrast to my memories of bustling streets and vibrant life. But it was also a symbol of resilience, of life's inherent ability to adapt and endure.

We spent the day exploring the city, navigating through its silent streets and abandoned buildings. Every corner held a story, every structure a testament to the past. But amidst the desolation, I also found fragments of hope. A resilient tree sprouting from the cracked pavement, a blooming flower amidst the rubble, a bird nesting in the skeletal remains of a building - all symbols of life thriving amidst the ruins.

As we ventured further into the city, we came across a playground. The sight of the rusty swings and the deserted sandpit brought a wave of nostalgia. I could almost hear the laughter of children, the chatter of parents, the buzz of a lively community. For a moment, I was no longer the last zombie, but a memory, a ghost of my former self.

We decided to camp for the night in an old school building nearby. As I settled down in the silence of the deserted classroom, my thoughts drifted to the children who once filled this space, their dreams, their hopes, their fears. The contrast between the past and the present was poignant, a grim reminder of the havoc wrought by the virus. And yet, in the midst of this bleak reality, I found solace. In the echoes of the past, in the resilience of the present, in the promise of the future.

AUGUST 31, YEAR UNKNOWN

Waking up in the abandoned school was a surreal experience. The empty desks, the dusty blackboard, the silent hallways - all bore silent testimony to the bustling activity that once filled these spaces.

Our exploration of the city continued. We found a library, its shelves still filled with books. They were dusty, some were damaged, but their presence filled me with a strange joy. Here was humanity's knowledge, its thoughts, its creativity, preserved amidst the ruins. I picked up a few, storing them in our backpack. They were not just books, they were fragments of a lost world, precious links to the past.

As we ventured further, we came across a hospital. Its white walls were now stained with time, windows broken, and the entrance was covered in overgrowth. But it was an undeniable sign of our past struggle to contain the outbreak. It was here that people sought treatment, hope, a chance at survival. It was a place of fear, of hope, of desperate battles between life and death.

The hospital was a chilling reminder of the scale of the devastation, of the millions of lives lost in the outbreak. As I stood there, looking at the crumbling structure, I felt a surge of determination. We were on the right path. We were moving closer to our goal, and with each passing day, the possibility of a cure, of salvation, was becoming more real.

As the sun set, we retreated to the school for the night. Today was a reminder of the world that was, of the

struggle that led us here, and of the hope that still persisted. I am the last zombie, and this is our journey.

SEPTEMBER 1, YEAR UNKNOWN

The morning brought a sense of unease. A storm had rolled in overnight, casting the city in a gloomy shade. As Rain and I ventured out into the city, the wind whistled through the deserted streets, creating an eerie symphony of hollow sounds. Today's goal was clear - search for supplies and any useful equipment.

We made our way towards what looked like a supermarket, the building's facade worn by time and neglect. Inside, shelves lay bare, long stripped of their contents. I remember how these places used to be full of life, people hustling, bustling, picking up their groceries for the week. Now, they stood as silent reminders of a time long gone.

Just as we were about to leave, Rain's ears perked up, her body going rigid. A low growl emanated from her, her eyes focused on the supermarket's back entrance. I strained my ears and heard it - a low rumbling sound, barely discernible but growing steadily louder. My heart pounded in my chest, a sense of dread settling in.

In a flash, a pack of wild dogs burst through the back entrance, snarling and baring their teeth. Their eyes were wild, bodies emaciated - creatures driven to desperation in this desolate world. My undead nature didn't deter them. Hunger, it seemed, overruled fear.

"Run, Rain!" I commanded, my voice barely a whisper. Rain needed no second bidding and darted off towards the entrance. I followed her, my feet carrying me faster than I thought possible. The dogs were close behind, their growls growing louder and more desperate.

We managed to evade them and took shelter in a nearby building. As the sounds of snarling faded into the distance, I slumped to the floor, a wave of relief washing over me. Rain whined softly, pressing her body against mine for comfort. I reassured her with gentle strokes, my own heart still pounding.

Today, the city showed us its other face - not just silent and desolate, but dangerous and unpredictable. We were safe for now, but today's encounter was a stark reminder of the risks we faced. Yet, in this post-apocalyptic world, every threat surmounted, every challenge overcome was another step towards survival, another testament to our resilience.

SEPTEMBER 2, YEAR UNKNOWN

After yesterday's close call, we decided to lay low. We spent the day inside the building we'd taken shelter in, listening to the storm rage outside. It was a bleak day, a fitting backdrop for the world we now found ourselves in. I found myself looking at Rain, her form curled up in a corner. We were survivors in this world, lone wanderers in a vast landscape of desolation.

I felt a profound connection with her, a shared understanding born out of our mutual survival. In this broken world, she was my companion, my confidante, my beacon of hope. The thought was comforting, a beacon of light in the surrounding darkness.

As the storm subsided, I found myself reflecting on our journey. The dangers we had faced, the challenges we had overcome, the hope that kept us going. I realized that despite the desolation, despite the bleakness, we had each other. In this world of ruins, amidst the echoes of a fallen civilization, we found companionship. We found hope. And in the end, wasn't that what survival was all about?

The storm had brought a chilling reminder of the reality we now faced. But it also brought a realization. We were stronger than we knew. We were survivors. And together, we would face whatever this world threw at us.

I am the last zombie, and this is our journey.

SEPTEMBER 3, YEAR UNKNOWN

The storm had cleared up and we emerged from our hideout with a renewed sense of purpose. After yesterday's close call, it was clear we needed to improve our defenses. I needed to find a weapon.

We set our sights on a nearby sporting goods store. Broken glass crunched under my feet as we entered, but inside, amidst the decay, lay a treasure trove of potential weapons. Baseball bats, hunting knives, even a few crossbows. I settled on a sturdy-looking aluminum baseball bat - lightweight yet solid. A few practice swings confirmed it felt right in my hand. Not an ideal weapon for a zombie, but it was something.

Meanwhile, Rain sniffed around, her nose leading her to a stash of camping food. Freeze-dried meals, energy bars, and a jackpot find - a few cans of dog food. Rain's tail wagged furiously as I popped open a can, her eager licks cleaning the can to a shine. I couldn't help but smile, watching her. In this dystopian reality, these small moments of joy felt magnified.

SEPTEMBER 4, YEAR UNKNOWN

After the necessities of food and protection were addressed, we ventured further into the city. My senses, heightened as they were, took in every detail - the way the sunlight hit the crumbling buildings, the soft rustle of wind through the desolate streets, the distant echoes of a world that was.

The city held stories in every corner, silent witnesses to the world we had lost. A coffee shop with cups still on the tables, a library with books left open, a school with art still displayed on its walls. Each scene held a poignant reminder of the vibrant life that once thrived here.

But in these remnants, I also found inspiration. The world had been devastated, but here were testaments of resilience, of the tenacity of life. These symbols of a fallen civilization also held within them the seeds of hope, a promise that life, though changed, persisted.

SEPTEMBER 5, YEAR UNKNOWN

We're making progress. The city, once intimidating in its desolation, was now becoming more familiar. We were learning its secrets, uncovering its stories, mapping its skeleton. Each day brought new discoveries, new challenges, and new reasons to continue.

Today, Rain found a toy in the ruins of a house - a small, squeaky rubber duck. She pranced around, a picture of joy in this grim landscape. Watching her, I was reminded that even in the face of adversity, there's always room for happiness, for moments of pure, unadulterated joy.

We're surviving. But more than that, we're living. Through the fear, the uncertainty, the challenges, we find reasons to go on, reasons to hope. Every day is a struggle, but every day is also a triumph - a testament to our resilience, our determination, our will to survive.

I am the last zombie, and this is our journey.

SEPTEMBER 6, YEAR UNKNOWN

The day started like any other. We were scoping the outskirts of the city, where the buildings thinned out and the vast, unexplored landscape lay before us. It was treacherous territory, with uneven ground and hidden dangers. As always, Rain led the way, her keen senses attuned to the subtlest signs of danger.

That's when I misjudged my footing. One moment, I was upright, the next, pain exploded in my ankle as I tumbled down a jagged slope. As an undead, I've grown somewhat numb to pain, but this... this was a raw, searing sensation that shot up my leg.

SEPTEMBER 7, YEAR UNKNOWN

The night had been long and restless, my leg throbbed incessantly. Rain whimpered at my side, sensing my discomfort. My ankle was swollen, a grotesque sight, even for a zombie. The situation was dire, I needed medical supplies.

SEPTEMBER 8, YEAR UNKNOWN

With Rain's help, I hobbled through the city, my eyes searching for the universal symbol of a cross. We had passed a few medical facilities on our explorations but I hadn't paid them much heed, until now. My injury was slowing us down, making us vulnerable.

SEPTEMBER 9, YEAR UNKNOWN

Today's journey was successful. We found an abandoned pharmacy, its shelves dusty, but still housing useful supplies. Antiseptic, bandages, painkillers – items that had been commonplace in the world before, now treasures in our dystopian reality. I cleaned and dressed the wound as best I could, while Rain kept watch.

SEPTEMBER 10, YEAR UNKNOWN

Despite the pain, there was a sense of satisfaction. The world had thrown yet another challenge our way, and we had faced it head on. The days were tough, but they were ours, filled with small victories and growing resilience. Each challenge weathered, each obstacle surmounted, brought us closer to our goal – survival.

My leg was still throbbing, but the wound was clean and bandaged. I was hoping that my zombie constitution would speed up the healing process. In the meantime, we would lay low and rest.

SEPTEMBER 11, YEAR UNKNOWN

The city lay still under the muted light of dawn. I found myself thinking about the world that was, about the bustling streets and busy lives that used to be. It was a world I was once part of, a world I once took for granted.

Now, it was all but a distant memory, a phantom echo in my mind. I looked down at my bandaged leg, a grim reminder of our present reality. Yet, despite the hardships, despite the challenges, I was still here. We were still here. And as long as we were, we would keep going, keep surviving.

I am the last zombie, and this is our journey.

SEPTEMBER 12, YEAR UNKNOWN

As the first light of day began to streak across the sky, I noticed a distant figure. At first, I thought my mind was playing tricks on me, the endless loneliness conjuring up phantoms. But as I squinted against the rising sun, I saw it - a human silhouette against the dusty horizon. It was moving slowly, but surely, in our direction. I immediately signaled to Rain, her ears perking up at the sense of urgency in my voice.

We spent the day in hiding, watching as the figure drew closer. As the hours passed, it became clear - we were being hunted. This was no random passerby, this was a human survivor, wary and dangerous. The sight of another living being should have filled me with hope, but instead, it brought fear. Humans, after all, were notorious for their prejudice against my kind.

SEPTEMBER 13, YEAR UNKNOWN

The hunter continued his slow pursuit today, always on the horizon, never straying too far. His presence was like a dark cloud, looming over us, casting a shadow on our journey. Our roles had reversed - I, the hunter, had become the hunted.

My injury made it impossible to confront or outrun him. We were trapped in this deadly game of cat and mouse, our survival hanging in the balance. The silence of the city seemed to amplify our predicament, each beat of my undead heart echoing with the impending danger. Rain too, felt the tension, her usual vibrant energy replaced by cautious vigilance.

SEPTEMBER 14, YEAR UNKNOWN

Despite the ever-present threat, we continued our struggle for survival. We scavenged for food, searched for better hiding spots, all the while keeping an eye on our pursuer.

Even in my current state, I couldn't help but wonder about this lone hunter. What was his story? What had he endured in this post-apocalyptic world? How had he survived when so many others hadn't? These questions haunted me, adding to the complex web of emotions I found myself tangled in.

Fear, curiosity, empathy - emotions that made me feel incredibly human, even in my undead state. It was a stark reminder of the intricate thread that connected all of us, the undying spirit of survival.

SEPTEMBER 15, YEAR UNKNOWN

Today, we found a relatively secure hiding spot - a basement under a demolished building. It was cold, damp, and filled with shadows. But it offered the one thing we needed the most - concealment.

We settled in, Rain curling up beside me, her warmth a comforting presence. As I gazed at the cracked ceiling, the hunter's silhouette never left my mind. He was out there, somewhere, his intentions unknown, his presence a constant reminder of our fragile existence.

Yet, as I looked down at Rain, her eyes closed in a fitful sleep, I found strength. We were survivors, against all odds. We had faced adversity, braved dangers, and were still here, still fighting. This was just another challenge, another hurdle to overcome.

I am the last zombie, and this is our journey.

SEPTEMBER 16, YEAR UNKNOWN

As dawn broke, I felt a wave of unease. I sat in our newfound sanctuary, a basement hidden beneath layers of rubble and decay, while Rain, ever faithful, rested at my side. She'd been skittish since we'd spotted the hunter, her canine instincts warning her of danger. Her behavior reinforced the growing sense of threat - the human, whoever they were, was a danger to us.

My mind swam with questions. Who was this person? How did they survive the fall of humanity? What drove them to hunt us, to chase down a zombie and a dog? Were they fearful, defensive, or just desperate? As a human, would they be sympathetic to my plight, or would they see only the undead monster I appeared to be?

SEPTEMBER 17, YEAR UNKNOWN

We ventured out of the basement today, under the gray skies of an overcast morning. It was a risk, but necessary. I was still healing, slower than I would've liked, but surviving nonetheless. Rain and I needed food and water, and we could not let the hunter dictate our lives entirely.

As we scavenged, I found my gaze continually drawn to the horizon, watching for any sign of our pursuer. My senses, heightened by my transformation, were on high alert. Each rustle of leaves, each creak of a derelict building, sent adrenaline coursing through me.

SEPTEMBER 18, YEAR UNKNOWN

We didn't see the hunter today. No figure on the horizon, no telltale signs of pursuit. It was eerily quiet, the city a desolate ghost of its former self. The silence was a stark reminder of our isolation. It was just Rain and me against the world - a world that had fallen, a world that had succumbed to the relentless march of the undead.

Even so, we pressed on. We found an old grocery store, its interior dark and foreboding. Inside, we discovered a trove of canned goods, long-life food items forgotten in the chaos. It felt like a small victory amidst the uncertainty. We took what we could carry and made our way back to our hideout.

SEPTEMBER 19, YEAR UNKNOWN

I spent the day nursing my ankle, the swollen flesh a mottled canvas of purple and black. It was an ugly reminder of my vulnerability, a stark contrast to the invulnerability I thought my undead state provided. My body, it seemed, had its limits.

The day slipped into evening, the world outside transitioning from hues of gray to the black of night. In the quiet, my mind wandered to the human hunter. Had they given up? Had they moved on, found other targets to pursue? Or were they out there, in the darkness, watching and waiting?

SEPTEMBER 20, YEAR UNKNOWN

Today, we planned. We couldn't continue living in fear, hiding from a threat that may or may not strike. We had to move forward, to seek out the promise of the Treatment Center that the old film reel had revealed. It was a beacon of hope in a world filled with darkness. A chance to find others like me, to prove that I was not alone, that I was not the last.

The hunter was still out there, but we could not let the fear of being hunted cripple us. We would remain vigilant, cautious, but we would not stop moving forward. After all, what was life, even in death, if not a ceaseless pursuit of hope?

SEPTEMBER 21, YEAR UNKNOWN

Today, the hunter made his move. We spotted him, not far from our hideout, his silhouette a grim specter against the fallen cityscape. He was closer than he'd ever been before, a sure sign that he was closing in. The sight of him, so close yet so far, sent a chill through my undead veins.

We watched him for what felt like an eternity, our breaths held, our hearts pounding. The tension was palpable, a heavy shroud that threatened to suffocate us. Rain growled softly beside me, her body tense, her gaze fixed on the looming threat.

It was a game of chicken, a deadly dance that could end in disaster. The hunter was testing us, gauging our reactions, searching for weaknesses. His patience was unsettling, a sign of his determination, his resolve.

SEPTEMBER 22, YEAR UNKNOWN

Our encounter yesterday got me thinking. It was clear the hunter was not going to give up. He was relentless, a predator in the truest sense. We were his prey, and he was closing in for the kill.

But I was not going to go down without a fight. No, I had to protect Rain, protect myself, and to do that, we needed a plan. So, as the sun rose today, casting long, eerie shadows across the desolate city, a plan began to take shape in my mind.

SEPTEMBER 23, YEAR UNKNOWN

Our plan was simple - set a trap for the hunter, incapacitate him, then make our escape. It wasn't foolproof, but it was the best we had. We had to assume the hunter was more experienced, more equipped, and more determined. But we had the element of surprise on our side, and we were going to use it to our advantage.

Today, we began laying the groundwork for our plan. We found an abandoned warehouse, its interior vast and labyrinthine, perfect for our needs. We spent the day setting up, turning the warehouse into a deadly maze filled with traps.

SEPTEMBER 24, YEAR UNKNOWN

With our trap set, all that was left was to lure the hunter in. Rain and I returned to our hideout, our movements deliberate and obvious. We wanted the hunter to see us, to follow us. It was risky, but necessary.

As night fell, we retreated to the warehouse, our hearts pounding in anticipation. Would the hunter take the bait? Would our plan work? We could only wait and hope.

SEPTEMBER 25, YEAR UNKNOWN

Today, our game of cat and mouse reached its climax. As dawn broke, we heard the hunter enter the warehouse. Each creak, each echo, was a testament to his presence. He was here, and our plan was in motion.

We watched from our hiding spot as the hunter navigated the labyrinth, his movements cautious and calculated. He was experienced, that much was clear. But we had the home field advantage, and we were not going down without a fight.

SEPTEMBER 26, YEAR UNKNOWN

The hunter was clever, I'll give him that. He avoided the first two traps, his keen eyes spotting the telltale signs. The first one was rather simple: a tripwire connected to a stack of heavy, unstable crates. The idea was that the hunter, upon entering the warehouse and presumably scouring the lower level, would trip the wire and send the crates toppling onto him. It was rudimentary, a trap born out of desperation and limited resources. But it was also effective, at least in theory.

We had positioned the tripwire strategically, hiding it amongst debris and fallen beams. But the hunter was not so easily fooled. He spotted the trap, either by seeing the wire or deducing the precariousness of the crates. He carefully stepped over the wire and continued his search, leaving the crates untouched.

Our second trap was more complex, a nod to the ingenuity that desperation can breed. We rigged up an old fire hose we'd found, attaching its nozzle to a pulley system we'd cobbled together. We'd then loaded the hose with all the rusty nails, broken glass, and other sharp debris we could find. The idea was to create a makeshift shotgun, a device that would blast the hunter with a deadly wave of shrapnel when triggered.

We positioned this trap on the warehouse's upper level, where we hoped the hunter would venture after avoiding the first trap. But, once again, the hunter proved his worth. He spotted the unusual setup, the fire hose conspicuously out of place amongst the warehouse's decay. He steered clear of the trap, leaving it unfired and us disappointed.
But he wasn't infallible, and he fell for the third one. A pit hidden beneath a layer of debris, a drop severe enough to incapacitate, but not kill.

We watched as he plummeted, his surprised yell echoing in the silent warehouse. Then, with our hearts pounding in our chests, we fled. We left the city behind, the hunter trapped and out of the way. Our plan had worked, against all odds, and for the first time in a long while, I felt hope stir within me.

SEPTEMBER 27, YEAR UNKNOWN

We're on the road now, leaving behind the city and the hunter. We've bought ourselves some time, but we can't rest on our laurels. The world is still a dangerous place, and we have a long journey ahead.

For now, though, we revel in our victory. We've outwitted a human, a testament to our survival instincts. But we're not out of the woods yet. The Treatment Center still looms large in our future, a beacon of hope in a world gone dark.

SEPTEMBER 28, YEAR UNKNOWN

Today marked our first full day away from the city. The looming buildings receded in the distance, becoming nothing more than a dark smudge against the horizon. The fear and tension that had clung to us in the city gradually gave way to a sense of cautious relief. We were on our own now, journeying into the unknown. The concrete jungle was replaced with fields of long-dead grass, the buzz of neon with the howl of the wind.

Rain and I trudged along, our path dictated by the sun's steady crawl across the sky. Despite the ordeal we'd just survived, there was no room for rest. We had to keep moving, keep putting distance between us and the city, between us and the hunter.

As the sun dipped below the horizon, painting the sky in shades of orange and red, we made camp. A patch of barren land offered a modicum of shelter from the elements, a small respite in an otherwise unforgiving world. We huddled together, Rain's fur warm against my cold skin, and watched as night fell.

With the darkness, though, came fresh fears. We had left the hunter behind, but there were other threats in this desolate world. Dogs. Once man's best friend, now turned into fearful predators, their minds warped by the virus just like mine. They roamed the wilderness in packs, their howls echoing through the night, a grim reminder of the world we now inhabited.

Rain seemed to sense my unease. She nestled closer, her small body trembling. I comforted her, my hand gently stroking her fur. She was scared, but so was I. We were alone in a world that was no longer ours, a world that was out to get us.

But we had each other, and for now, that was enough. Tomorrow, we would continue our journey. The Treatment Center was still out there, somewhere, waiting for us. But for now, we huddled together against the chill, staring out into the darkness, our hearts beating in unison, our hopes intertwined. We were survivors. We were fighters. And we were not going down without a fight.

SEPTEMBER 29, YEAR UNKNOWN

This morning started with an unexpected encounter. A group of soldiers, or what passed for them now, were chasing a young woman through the fields. Their cruel laughter echoed in the air, a stark contrast to her terrified silence.

Without a second thought, Rain and I sprang into action. The dog's growl was a low rumble in her chest, a primal warning to those who dared threaten us or ours. I was reminded of my own unnatural strength, a side-effect of the virus that turned me. I could feel my body yearning to protect, to save. But it was not a selfless act. It was instinct, a need to keep my pack safe.

The fight was brutal. I fell upon the soldiers like a wild animal, my hands weapons, my strength formidable. They fell one by one, their last moments filled with shock and fear. They had been the predators, but now they were the prey.

After it was over, I stood panting heavily, surrounded by the aftermath of my actions. The woman, shaking and mute, was staring at me with wide eyes. She was afraid, understandably so, but also intrigued. She held out her hand, offering a silent thanks, but quickly recoiled when she saw the inhuman hunger flicker in my eyes.

We left her there, in the middle of the field, with the bodies of the soldiers scattered around her. But as we trudged away, I noticed her shadow flitting behind us. She was keeping her distance, wary and scared, but she was following us nonetheless.

The day ended with a bitter taste in my mouth. I had saved a life, yes, but at what cost? I was reminded of my own monstrous nature, of the power and savagery that came with being a creature of the virus. The lines between man and beast were blurred, and I was treading a fine balance. Would I eventually lose myself to the monster within?

As we huddled together under the stars, the three of us lost in our own thoughts, I couldn't help but hope that the Treatment Center held answers. That it could offer me a semblance of humanity, a chance to keep the beast at bay. The girl was now a part of our strange family, another soul entrusting her survival to us.

The world might be a dangerous place, but as long as we had each other, we stood a chance. With a sigh, I closed my eyes, the haunting image of today's violence etched into my memory. Tomorrow, we would press on. For Rain. For the girl. For our survival.

SEPTEMBER 30, YEAR UNKNOWN

In the harsh light of dawn, our world was a stark tableau of survival, a bleak picture painted in broad strokes of hope and despair. We roused from our rest, Rain's soft whines stirring me from a dreamless sleep. My joints creaked in protest as I stretched, but there was no time for complaints. We had to keep moving.

The girl, as silent as ever, kept her distance, trailing behind us like a cautious specter. Her eyes were wide, flitting nervously from me to Rain, and then back again. I could see the fear in her gaze, but also a glimmer of reluctant trust. It was a start, I supposed.

As the day wore on, we stumbled upon a desolate playground, an eerie reminder of a time when laughter and joy filled the air, a stark contrast to the hushed whispers of the wind that now echoed through the rusted swings and faded slides. It was a haunting scene, one that made my unbeating heart ache with a sense of longing.

I watched as Rain bounded around the area, her tail wagging furiously. The sight brought a rare smile to my face. The dog had an uncanny ability to find joy even in the bleakest situations, a trait I admired and envied in equal measure.

The girl watched us from a safe distance, her guarded demeanor slowly thawing as she watched our playful display. I could see the faintest hint of a smile tugging at the corners of her mouth. It was a small victory, but a victory nonetheless.

As night fell, we found shelter in an abandoned bus near the playground. It was cramped and uncomfortable, but it offered protection from the elements and a vantage point to watch out for any threats.

We settled in, the silence of the night broken only by the occasional howls in the distance. The girl sat across from us, her back pressed against the cold metal wall of the bus. She was still quiet, her silence a fortress she had built around herself.

Today was a day of small victories and harsh reminders of the world we were living in. We might have come together under strange circumstances, but we were now a team, bound by our will to survive.

As I drifted off to sleep, the sight of the deserted playground imprinted on my mind, I couldn't help but think about the world we'd lost and the world we were fighting to survive in. Tomorrow was another day, another step towards our destination.

OCTOBER 1, YEAR UNKNOWN

I was jerked out of my sleep by a shaking hand. The girl's wide, frightened eyes met mine. A low rumbling filled the air, the unmistakable growl of engines. Rain was gone. The bus was trembling subtly with each engine rev. And suddenly, my mind was a whirlwind of thoughts, all revolving around one pressing question: where was Rain?

"Stay here," I whispered, gesturing for the girl to stay put as I moved towards the broken window, peeking out. Outside, I saw the dark shapes of vehicles, their lights cutting through the early morning fog. They were just outlines in the haze, but the menace they radiated was palpable.

Fear seized me, a cold vice around my heart. Not for myself, but for Rain. I'd seen the girl was brave, but Rain was vulnerable, just a small creature in a world too large and too cruel.

"Stay," I repeated to the girl, pressing my finger to my lips. She nodded, her gaze never leaving my face. I crept out of the bus, my every sense heightened, my heart pounding against my ribs.

I was careful to stick to the shadows, moving silently despite my growing panic. The vehicles were closer now, and I could see they were military trucks, armed and armored. But who drove them? Was it another group of rogue soldiers? Hunters?

My thoughts were interrupted by a soft whine. Rain. The sound came from behind one of the trucks. I moved closer, my heart pounding louder with each step.

Then I saw her. Rain was hidden behind some crates, her little body shivering, her eyes wide and terrified. But she was okay. She was safe. Relief washed over me like a wave, but there was no time to celebrate. We had to leave before whoever drove those trucks found us.

With Rain in my arms, I retreated, moving as quickly and silently as I could back towards the bus. The girl was waiting, her face pale but determined. She didn't scream, didn't cry out. She just opened her arms to take Rain, holding the trembling dog close.

We left the bus behind, slipping away into the pre-dawn light, the growl of the engines a haunting lullaby in our wake. As the adrenaline wore off, the reality of the situation hit me. We were being hunted, our peaceful morning shattered in an instant. And I had no idea who our hunters were, or what they wanted.

But for now, we were safe. And we were together. That was all that mattered. With the girl and Rain by my side, I was ready to face whatever came our way. And face it we would. Because we were survivors, each in our own way. And we would not go down without a fight.

OCTOBER 2, YEAR UNKNOWN

This morning started with a ray of sunlight. Not just because the weather was good - clear blue skies above us for once - but because of the girl. For the first time since we met, she voluntarily interacted with me, her brave but silent guardian.

She pulled out a tattered doll from her bag, its porcelain face smudged with dirt, its glass eyes vacant but somehow haunting. She hugged the doll close, then turned to me and tried to form a word. Her mouth struggled with the shape of it, her voice barely a whisper.

"Baby?" she mouthed again, pointing at the doll. I cocked my head, trying to understand. I wasn't sure what she meant. Was the doll her baby? Or was she trying to tell me something else?

Seeing my confusion, her brows furrowed, and she gestured again, more urgently this time. But the word remained elusive, dancing on the tip of her tongue but never quite making it out. Frustration flared in her eyes, and she retreated back into her silence, hugging the doll close.

The rest of the day was spent on the move. We had to put as much distance between ourselves and those trucks as possible. With Hope leading the way, we traversed across the barren landscapes, our feet kicking up clouds of dust.

As we walked, I couldn't help but wonder about the girl's doll. Was it a token from her past? A reminder of a time when she could speak, when her world wasn't filled with nightmares? Or was it something more? A symbol of her longing for a normal life, a semblance of innocence in this cruel world?

Despite the good weather, a cloud hung over us. The frustration from our failed communication lingered, but I knew we couldn't let it break us. We had to learn to understand each other if we were to survive. For now, the sound of our footfalls and the rhythm of our breaths were the only conversation we needed.

Tonight, as we camp in the shelter of an old gas station, I watch the girl as she cradles her doll, her face softened by the moonlight. I hope that tomorrow will bring us closer to understanding each other. We are all we've got in this world, and together, we will face the unknown.

OCTOBER 3, YEAR UNKNOWN

I woke up to emptiness. The spot where the girl had been sleeping was bare, her doll the only proof of her presence. My heart clenched at the sight. After everything, how could she just disappear without a word?

Except she had left a word. On the dusty surface of the old gas station's mirror, she'd traced a word with her finger. "Baby". The same word she had tried so desperately to say. I stared at it, the letters stark and harsh in the dim light. But what did it mean?

Frustration gnawed at me, followed swiftly by concern. The girl was alone, vulnerable. She had enemies and she couldn't even call for help. I couldn't let her face whatever was out there by herself. She might not have asked for my protection, but I had given it freely. I wouldn't abandon her now.

So I decided to follow her. The grand plan of uncovering the secrets in the old movie reel would have to wait. This girl needed me. And if I'm being honest, I needed her, too. Her silent strength, her unyielding determination; they gave me hope. Rain for something beyond survival.

I took Rain, my ever-faithful companion, and set her to the task of tracking the girl. The dog's senses were far sharper than mine and I trusted her with all I had. She sniffed the air, then the ground where the girl had slept, then the air again. Her tail wagged slowly as she picked up the scent and then, without a look back, she bounded off.

We trekked through the desolate landscape, following Rain's lead. My mind was a whirlwind of worry and questions. Where was the girl going? Was she in trouble? What did "baby" mean?

As the day bled into evening, I realized I had been fooling myself. The girl was not just some stranger I had saved. She had become a part of my strange little family. And I wouldn't give up on family.

Tonight, I'm following a trail under the stars, Rain by my side, my heart heavy but determined. I will find her. I will make sure she's safe. And maybe, just maybe, I will understand what "baby" means.

OCTOBER 4, YEAR UNKNOWN

The sun has risen, casting long shadows over the cracked asphalt and abandoned buildings. Rain's nose is to the ground, her ears perked high, listening to the silence as we move. The world feels empty without the girl. My heart aches as I cradle the doll in my hands, the porcelain cold, the glass eyes vacant.

Why did she leave it? Was it a clue for me to follow? A sign she would return? Or maybe she was just done with it, done with trying to communicate something I couldn't understand.

My mind spins with these questions, each one burrowing deeper, making the constant ache in my head even worse. I remember when my mind was sharp, filled with knowledge and clarity. But now it feels fogged over, like trying to peer through a dirty window. It's a slow, gradual frustration that builds and churns in the pit of my gut.

I'm not like the others, the ones who had been bitten. The walking corpses that once roamed the streets. I was different. I was...smarter, somehow. But I hadn't been bitten, no. I had just become.

It hurts to think about it. The past is a jumble of images, of words and faces that no longer make sense. Sometimes, I can almost grasp a fragment of my former life, but it slips through my fingers, like sand on a windy day.

The girl's sudden departure has stirred these thoughts, brought them bubbling up to the surface. I don't want to think about it, about who I was or what happened. It's too painful. I'm not that person anymore.

I'm just Lance now. Just a zombie trying to survive, trying to keep his little family safe. That's all that matters. Not my past, not my identity. Just survival.

The day passes in silence. We walk, Rain's nose sniffing out the trail, my eyes scanning the horizon for any sign of the girl. But there's nothing. Just the echoing silence of a world that no longer is.

Tonight, as I sit under the stars, the doll beside me, I can't help but feel a sense of loss. A loss of the girl, yes, but also a loss of who I was, of the life I can't remember. I clutch the doll tighter and make a silent promise to myself - I will find her, and maybe in doing so, find a piece of myself too.

OCTOBER 5, YEAR UNKNOWN

This morning, as we crested a small hill, a town spread out before us, nestled in a valley between craggy mountain peaks. It was not the silent, ghostly cityscape I was used to. Instead, this town bore signs of life, or at least, recent activity. Shreds of clothes flapping on makeshift lines, hints of smoke lingering in the air, footprints in the dirt that were too fresh to have been washed away by the elements.

The sight set my nerves on edge. This place was...inhabited. By whom or what, I couldn't say, but something about it made the hair on the back of my neck stand up. My first instinct was to skirt around it, to find a safer route, but the towering mountains were a forbidding barrier.

I turned to Rain, searching for reassurance. Her nose was to the ground, her ears alert. I saw her sniff the air and then turn to me, her eyes bright. She was telling me that the girl's scent led into the town.

So, we had no choice. We would have to go through. A surge of adrenaline coursed through my veins. Danger or no, this was the path she had taken. And I was not about to abandon our mission, not after everything we had been through.

I gazed out at the town, steeling myself for the challenge ahead. Every instinct told me that danger lurked within those borders, that the silent houses and deserted streets hid threats we were yet to encounter. But we had faced threats before. We would face them again. For the girl, for our family, we would walk into the lion's den.

Tonight, we make camp at the town's edge, under the shadow of the mountains. Tomorrow, we step into unknown territory. Tomorrow, we continue our pursuit, regardless of the danger that awaits. The moon shines down on us, a silent guardian in the dark. I look at it, at the countless stars dotting the night sky, and I make a promise, to the girl, to myself, to Rain. We will find her. And we will stay together, no matter what.

OCTOBER 6, YEAR UNKNOWN

I woke today with a gnawing hunger, a deep, primal urge that caused my heart to quicken and my body to tremble. It wasn't a hunger for food; I haven't had a meal in as long as I can remember. I don't need sustenance, not the kind humans need anyway. But this hunger... it was something else. It was a desire, a longing for something I couldn't quite comprehend, and it filled me with fear.

Rain must have sensed my distress because she hovered around me, whining softly. I tried to calm myself, to shake off the gnawing hunger, but it clung to me like a second skin. With a heavy heart, we moved on, entering the town with a shared apprehension.

It all fell apart in an instant. The town, seemingly desolate at first, came alive in the most horrifying way. We barely made it past the first few houses when we were ambushed. Figures swarmed from the buildings, from the narrow alleys, their faces masks of hostility.

These weren't the shambling husks I was familiar with. These were survivors, humans who had somehow managed to resist the infection, to outlive the apocalypse. They wielded crude weapons - shovels, metal rods, anything they could find, and they bore down on us with a frenzied determination.

Rain growled, her fur bristling, ready to defend us. But I was frozen. The sight of living, breathing humans was as surprising as it was terrifying. The last time I had encountered a group of survivors, things hadn't ended well. I didn't want a repeat of that.

The hunger roiled within me, growing stronger, more insistent. I could feel my control slipping, the human part of me retreating to the shadows. Panic welled up, threatening to consume me. I had to fight it. I had to stay in control.

But then a stone hit me square in the chest, another scratched Rain, and all bets were off. The world blurred as the animal within me took over. The screams of the survivors filled the air, but they were a distant echo, drowned out by the roaring hunger in my veins.

Tonight, I write with trembling hands. We are hiding in one of the abandoned houses on the outskirts of town. The survivors are still searching for us, their angry voices a grim reminder of our predicament. I feel... different. Changed. The hunger has subsided, but the fear remains.

My body aches, my mind spins with the day's events, but one thing is clear. We have to leave this town, find another route, another way. The girl... I hope she is safe, I hope she managed to slip past these survivors. I will not rest until I find her. No matter what it takes, no matter the cost, I will find her.

OCTOBER 7, YEAR UNKNOWN

The dawn was tinged with a sense of urgency as we quietly fled the refuge of the abandoned house, leaving behind the town and its hostile inhabitants. My body felt leaden with exhaustion, but the events of yesterday had lit a fire of determination in me. We had to get away, to put as much distance between us and the town as possible.

Rain seemed to echo my sentiments. She led the way with a wary alertness, her nose to the ground, tracking the faint scent of the girl. We moved in silence, the only sound being the crunch of dried leaves under our feet and the distant cries of birds.

My mind was a whirlwind of worry and regret. Had we made the right choice in coming to this town? Did we jeopardize our mission, and the girl, by being reckless? These thoughts haunted me, gnawing at my conscience as we trekked through the wilderness.

The encounter with the survivors had left a bitter taste in my mouth. The sight of their hostile faces, the weapons raised in fear and hatred, was a stark reminder of what I had become. A monster, a creature of the night that was to be feared and hunted. The hunger had been a terrifying experience, one I was afraid would happen again.

By the time the sun began to dip below the horizon, we had covered a good distance. We found a dense grove of trees offering some cover, and decided to camp for the night. I write these words by the dying light, Rain by my side, the silent darkness enveloping us.

Today was a painful reminder of our predicament, of the world we live in. But it was also a reaffirmation of our resolve. We have a mission, a purpose. We have someone to find, to protect. We are alone, but we are not helpless. We will continue our journey, no matter what obstacles stand in our way.

Tomorrow, we venture deeper into the wilderness, following the faint trace of the girl. The road ahead is uncertain, filled with potential dangers. But we press on. For the girl. For us. For a future that is more than just survival.

OCTOBER 8, YEAR UNKNOWN

The day's travel led us to an old service station, a decrepit structure swallowed by overgrown vegetation and the ravages of time. The rusted hulk of a car sat lonesomely near the crumbling pumps, its once vibrant paint now a faded memory.

Rain stopped suddenly, sniffing the air with a sense of confusion. Her tail dropped, ears flattening against her head as she approached the concrete forecourt, her usually relentless pace slowing down. The trail, it seemed, had gone cold here. I scanned the surroundings, the sinking feeling in my gut deepening as I saw the fresh puddle of fuel beneath one of the decaying pumps. A glint of metal near it caught my eye - a small trinket, a charm that had been on the girl's wrist.

I swallowed hard, my thoughts racing. Could the girl have been here? The sight of the charm and the fresh fuel puddle painted a disconcerting picture. Had she been taken? Or worse? The weight of our mission seemed heavier in the face of this chilling discovery.

I found myself pacing around the service station, my mind working on overdrive. We had to be faster, smarter, and more vigilant. The idea of the girl in harm's way, potentially caught up in the brutal reality of this harsh world was a potent motivator.

I decided then and there - we needed to quicken our pace, to find her before it was too late. But how? Traveling by foot through this treacherous terrain was slow and taxing. And then, my gaze landed on the decrepit car by the pumps.

Suddenly, it wasn't just a rusted hulk anymore. It was a potential vessel, a means of accelerating our pursuit. Could it be made to run again? I was no mechanic, but I knew basic stuff, bits and pieces picked up from a previous life. Could those memories serve me now in my hour of need?

As the sun sets, I write this entry in the faint glow of the service station's flickering lights. Tomorrow, we work on the car. Tonight, I plan, strategize, hope. We're not out of this yet. We will find her. We must.

OCTOBER 9, YEAR UNKNOWN

Today was a day of trials and tribulations. As the sun rose, I set to work on the car with a renewed sense of purpose. But life, it seems, has a cruel sense of humor.

I was prying open the fuel cap when the smell hit me. The pungent odor of petrol, raw and heady. For a moment, it was nothing more than an unpleasant smell. But then, the world tilted. A wave of dizziness washed over me. My head pounded as if my skull was trying to burst open. I slumped to the ground, my body convulsing in violent spasms. Rain, alarmed, barked incessantly, nuzzling her head against my chest.

It was a seizure, the first of its kind. A new torment to add to my cursed existence. Once the wave of pain receded, I was left gasping for air, my body soaked in cold sweat. I knew then, the fumes were too potent for my system. I would need some sort of protection if I were to continue working on the vehicle.

We found an old farmhouse not far from the service station. It stood alone, an island amidst a sea of overgrown fields. It was a beacon of hope. Maybe we could find some sort of mask or cloth to cover my mouth and nose, to filter the offending fumes.

As we approached, Rain took the lead, her nose to the ground, sniffing for any signs of danger. The door creaked ominously as we pushed it open, revealing a home frozen in time. Dust blanketed everything, a clear sign of its abandonment.

We searched through the dusty rooms, uncovering the remnants of lives once lived. Old photographs, moth-eaten clothes, broken china. A soft whine from Rain drew my attention to a small room at the back. It was a child's room, with faded murals on the walls and a small wooden chest filled with toys. Among them, a superhero mask, likely a beloved possession of a child long gone.

As I write this entry under the moonlight, the mask lies next to me. It's a crude solution, but it might just work. Tomorrow, we return to the car. We continue our mission, the seizure a stark reminder of the urgency. I can't afford to falter, to give in to the despair. We must press on. For her. For us. For survival.

OCTOBER 10, YEAR UNKNOWN

Today's entry is of minor victories and greater frustrations. The superhero mask proved its worth, allowing me to brave the harsh fumes for a while. It was a strange sight, I'm sure: a decayed, shambling being tinkering with a car, donning a brightly colored mask intended for children's games.

The work was laborious, physically demanding, but these trials were well within my capabilities. Lifting heavy car parts, pushing and pulling machinery – these were the tasks that made sense, that didn't torment me. After all, physical strength is a perk that comes with my curse.

But then came the need for delicacy, precision – human traits that I'd lost somewhere along the way. The task of removing a spark plug seemed insurmountable. Its stubborn refusal to yield to my clumsy, monstrous strength was an unnerving reminder of my limitations.

I struggled with the spark plug for what seemed like hours, the frustration gnawing at me. It was a small, insignificant thing, yet its defiance made it a symbol of everything I was fighting against: my affliction, my loneliness, my loss of humanity.

In the end, it was Rain who provided a distraction, finding a stick and dropping it at my feet, wagging her tail in that playful manner she has. The stick was a gnarled piece of wood, worn smooth by weather and time. It sparked an idea in my clouded mind.

I took a piece of cloth and wrapped it around the stick, creating a makeshift tool. It was crude, far from perfect, but it allowed me to apply the leverage and precision needed to remove the spark plug. The relief was palpable, a surge of triumph in a day filled with frustration.

Tonight, as I reflect on today's trials, I realize that it's these minor victories that keep me going, that give me hope. Hope... such a strange concept for a being like me. But as long as I draw breath, as long as there's a flicker of life within me, I will not surrender to despair.

Tomorrow, we continue our work on the car. Tomorrow, we continue our search. The mask will be my shield, my rag-wrapped stick, my weapon. Against the odds, against my own nature, I am fighting, living, surviving. It's all I can do.

OCTOBER 11, YEAR UNKNOWN

The dawn was colored with omens. Dark, bloated clouds scudded across the sky, promising a tempest. The air was heavy with electric anticipation. The wind, carrying an apocalyptic portent, moaned through the skeletal remains of the town.

I know what thunderstorms are, I remember their science. I know it's just the atmosphere rebelling, charged particles clashing in a titanic struggle. But there is a primitive part of me that trembles at the raw fury of nature unleashed. There's a disquiet in my bones that mirrors the roiling sky, an unease that transcends logic.

Rain seemed to share my dread, her usual energetic demeanour muted. She stayed close, her warm body pressed against my cold one. Our work on the car was stalled. The impending storm made it unwise to tinker with the volatile fuel. We had to abandon it and retreat to the farmhouse.

The farmhouse, a derelict edifice barely standing, offered a grim sort of shelter. It creaked and groaned under the assault of the wind, each moan a testament to its years of neglect. We huddled in a corner, Rain's nervous whines barely audible over the howl of the storm. I held her close, my hand automatically stroking her fur in an attempt to comfort her, and perhaps, myself.

That's when I felt it. A cool draft coming from the wooden floor beneath us. Probing the planks with my fingers, I found a loose one. After prying it open, a hidden cellar revealed itself. A jumble of items lay in the dim, dusty space below, a hoard of a bygone era. But there, amongst the debris, was an item that brought a glimmer of hope: a well-stocked first-aid kit.

It was a curious mix of emotions, this discovery. I stared at the bandages, the antiseptics, the medications - relics from a time when such things mattered. To me, they were redundant; my body doesn't heal the way it used to. But there was an undeniable relief too. If we were to encounter another human, another situation like the girl, we would have resources now. We could help, really help.

Tonight, as the storm rages outside, I find myself holding onto that hope, that chance of redemption. The storm will pass, and so too will this phase of darkness within me. In the echoes of the thunder, I hear the heartbeat of a world that refuses to die. And as long as that heartbeat endures, so shall I.

OCTOBER 12, YEAR UNKNOWN

What an irony. All this while, I was craving water. Today, I am cursing it. The car, our hope of catching up with the girl, is all but lost. The storm raged last night, its anger unrestrained, and the floodwaters have claimed the gas tank.

All my work, all my struggling with plugs and wires, just washed away. What hurts more, though, is the realization that it's my fault. I left the car exposed, didn't take the necessary precautions, got overwhelmed by my irrational fear of the storm. My mind...it betrays me again.

My hands, once dextrous and sure, fumbled and failed me yesterday. Now, my mind, once a beacon of intellect and clarity, stumbles in the foggy abyss of forgetfulness and fear. It's a torment, this relentless attrition of self.

Every step I take, every day I survive, the fog in my mind thickens. The world around me blurs. The clarity, the purpose that I cling to, it's slipping away, one terrifying moment at a time. I'm left grappling, clawing at the crumbling edges of my consciousness, desperate to hold onto the fragments of my humanity. But the fog is unrelenting, smothering, and I feel...lost.

Rain watches me, her intelligent eyes full of a concern that rips through me. I can almost hear her whimpering, the silent plea in her gaze. "Hold on," she seems to say. "Hold on, because I can't do this without you."

So I hold on. I clutch my frustration, my despair, and I lock it away. I have to find a way to push through this fog, to dispel it, to reclaim my mind. It's not just about surviving anymore; it's about retaining the essence of who I was, who I still am beneath this cursed existence.

Today, we go back to the farmhouse. We take stock of our resources, we plan, we strategize. We keep moving forward.

Because that's all we can do. That's all I can do.

I am the last zombie, but I am also Lance. And Lance does not give up.

OCTOBER 13, YEAR UNKNOWN

Desperation can turn even the most absurd notions into possibilities. As a kid, I remember reading stories of cowboys, their wild rides across the vast American plains, their gritty duels, their unyielding bond with their horses. It felt like fiction then, worlds apart from the world I knew. But today, I am going back to those stories.

I need to go back to the town. Not for the danger that lurks in every corner, not for the lurking hunters or the scavengers, but for a horse. The image of a cowboy on his horse, silhouetted against the setting sun, has transformed from a figment of fiction to a beacon of hope for me.

Rain seems unsure, her eyes darting nervously between me and the road leading back to town. I don't blame her. The last time we were there, things went terribly wrong. The fact that we escaped unscathed was nothing short of a miracle. But we have to risk it. We have no other choice.

So we set off, leaving behind the abandoned car, the ruined gas station, and the farmhouse that served as our temporary haven. I can feel the cold hand of fear tightening its grip around my heart as we near the town, the signs of decay and destruction stark reminders of the world we're living in.

I walk ahead, Rain trotting cautiously behind me, her sharp senses alert to every sound, every movement. I feel a sense of deja vu, a familiar dread creeping up my spine, but I force myself to move forward.

There's a stable on the outskirts of the town, a relic of an era long gone, a shadow of its former self. I vaguely remember seeing it on our way out. That's our destination. That's where we hope to find our escape. A horse. A living, breathing creature that could help us traverse this treacherous landscape.

I am the last zombie, venturing into a den of death for a glimmer of life. It feels surreal, but it's my reality. And I need to make it count. For the girl, for Rain, for me.

Tonight, we camp in the outskirts of the town, under the skeletal remains of an old bridge. I sit in the semi-darkness, Rain snuggled close, the silence of the night broken only by the occasional howl in the distance. As I close my eyes, I see the image of the cowboy again, his silhouette merging with mine. Tomorrow, I hope to live that image. Tomorrow, I hope to find our horse.

OCTOBER 14, YEAR UNKNOWN

The stable, much like everything else in this town, was a disappointing echo of the past. The horse we had pinned our hopes on was already on death's door. It lay on its side, its ribs pressing out against its skin, eyes hollowed with pain and neglect. A fractured leg, a brutal testament of its last struggle for survival, lay twisted awkwardly. The stench of neglect, of unclean drinking water, and the crushing silence of forgotten existence, hung heavy in the air. I felt a surge of anger towards its owners, the supposed custodians of this beautiful creature. Where were they now?

My thoughts were interrupted by a loud bang, a searing pain across my chest, and Rain's terrified yelp. The owner of the horse, a man of grotesque size, his once white shirt stretched to its limit against his bulging stomach, stood at the entrance of the stable, his face twisted into a malevolent grin.

He aimed his gun at Rain next, cocking it for another shot. His laugh echoed around the stable, a terrifying sound that filled me with a primal rage. My own pain was secondary, but the threat against Rain was unacceptable. I lunged at him, my hands closing around his neck, his laughter morphing into a gurgled cry. His eyes widened with fear as I tightened my grip, his gun slipping from his trembling fingers. I didn't mean to break his neck, but I did.

In the eerie silence that followed, I heard the horse take its last shuddering breath. An idea, crazy but tantalising, flashed through my mind. I bit the horse. Would the virus take? Could this be another chance for this poor, neglected creature? But nothing happened.

Disheartened, we left the stable and took shelter in the man's cabin as another storm raged outside. The day had been a rollercoaster of hope and disappointment, and all I could do was hope that tomorrow would bring a better tide. As we settled in for the night, the harsh reality of our world set in deeper - hope is a luxury, survival is the only necessity. And yet, we keep hoping, don't we?

OCTOBER 15, YEAR UNKNOWN

The breaking dawn did nothing to dispel the chill in my bones. Sleep was fitful at best, my dreams a twisted blend of fears and hopes. But then, an unfamiliar sound roused me from my uneasy slumber. The rhythmic clip-clop of hooves, the soft nicker of a horse. I jolted awake, disbelief etched into my face.

There, in the doorway of the cabin, stood the horse.

Alive. Awake. In the house.

But it wasn't just alive. It looked good. Strong. Its eyes held the same otherworldly glow as mine, its skin adorned with the unmistakable hue of our kind. It was alive, yes, but not as a dying, forgotten creature. It was alive as one of us. As a zombie.

I couldn't help it. I laughed. The sound echoed in the silent cabin, a joyous, incredulous, relieved laugh. I was ecstatic, and not because I had a new means of transportation, but because I had saved this beautiful creature. Given it another chance, another shot at life.

The horse stared at me, its eyes a mirror to my own – intelligent, curious, and carrying the quiet strength of a survivor. A new member of our small, strange family.

Rain, curious and cautious, ventured closer to the horse, her tail wagging in slow, friendly arcs. There was a sense of acceptance in her approach, a welcoming of the new member. I watched as she and the horse tentatively sniffed each other, an introduction of sorts.

In that moment, I felt a surge of happiness. It wasn't much, but it was a victory nonetheless. And in our world, every small victory mattered. Today was a good day, a day of hope and survival, a day of laughter and introductions, a day of life.

OCTOBER 16, YEAR UNKNOWN

Riding a horse that has experienced the change like I have is nothing short of surreal. It seems the horse, which Rain and I have now decided to call Thunder, is having a difficult time adjusting to his new... state. Thunder, aptly named for his renewed vibrance and zest, has a love for speed. And the desire to stop... not so much.

We started our day trying to make a saddle from the dead man's leathery jackets, a makeshift bridle from some ragged ropes. I mounted him with a sense of anticipation. His flesh, cold beneath me, his eyes glowing with that same eerie light, it was as if I was looking at myself, experiencing what I was from another perspective.

The moment Thunder's hooves struck the dusty ground in a canter, I knew we were in for a wild ride. The exhilaration was instantaneous. Wind ripping through what's left of my hair, the rapid, rhythmic beats of hooves drumming against the earth, the sheer thrill of it was intoxicating. Thunder loved to run. He relished it. His strides were long, his movements fluid. It was as if he was made for this – made for the wild abandon of an unfettered gallop.

The problem arose when it was time to stop. Thunder, in his newfound state, seemed to forget that stopping was a part of the journey. Or perhaps he just didn't want to. I pulled at the reins, my voice lost to the wind, but it was futile. He ran and ran until finally, his energy drained, he slowed down, panting and shaking.

It took some trial and error, some adjustments on my part and a bit of patience, but by nightfall, we had a system in place. A sort of understanding, you could say. Thunder would run, and I would let him, for a while. But when I needed him to stop, he would have to. It was a compromise, one that I hoped would work out in the long run.

As I sat by the dying embers of the fire that night, Thunder standing guard by me, Rain curled up at my feet, I couldn't help but feel a sense of camaraderie. We were different, all of us, changed by this world, but together, we were a family. A zombie, a horse, and a dog. Quite the picture we painted. But it was our reality. And for the moment, it was enough.

OCTOBER 17, YEAR UNKNOWN

Today, as we journeyed further, following the trail that seemed to wind endlessly, I found my mind consumed with a thought. A puzzle that was as intriguing as it was perplexing. What makes Rain and the girl so different? What allows them to accept a creature like me, a zombie, when the rest of their kind fear and detest us? Even Rain, the loyal canine that she is, seemed to take Thunder's new state in stride, curiously sniffing around him, wagging her tail, engaging in a peculiar kind of friendship.

As we trotted along, I watched Rain and Thunder interact. There was an understanding, an acceptance that defied my comprehension. Here was a dog, one of the most intuitive creatures, befriending a being that she should naturally be terrified of. And not just me, but now Thunder too. What made her so different? Was it her prolonged exposure to my kind, or was there something more? Some intrinsic ability to see beyond the ghastly exterior, to recognize the essence of what once was?

Then there was the girl. Silent and frightened, yet choosing to stay close to us despite having ample opportunities to escape. It was clear she had suffered at the hands of her own species. Perhaps it was that pain, that betrayal which allowed her to see us differently. After all, we had saved her. But was that enough to wipe away the inherent fear of the grotesque?

I remember my own transformation. The agony of it, the confusion. I remember looking at my reflection, seeing the monster I had become, feeling the revulsion course through me. But over time, that horror has lessened. I have accepted what I am, or at least, learned to live with it. Is it so inconceivable then, that others can do the same?

I pondered these questions as we journeyed, each one opening up a cascade of new ones. It's funny, I used to think that becoming a zombie meant losing your ability to think, to question, to feel. But here I am, a walking paradox. An abomination to some, a protector to others, and a philosopher to myself.

As night descended, I found myself no closer to the answers. Perhaps I never will be. But for now, that's okay. For now, I have Rain, I have Thunder, and somewhere out there, I hope, the girl. And for now, that's enough.

Sleep, for my kind, is a strange thing. We don't need it, not like humans do. But there are times when the mind, perhaps from some remnant of its human past, drifts into a hazy oblivion. Not quite sleep, but a state of dormant consciousness, a state that sometimes, if I'm unfortunate enough, brings forth dreams.

Last night, I was once again the captive of my subconscious. A parade of disjointed images, fears, and memories played out in the theater of my mind. I found myself on a battlefield, gunfire echoing in the distance. The stench of blood and gunpowder filled the air. I was a soldier, decked out in military fatigues, my hands wielding a rifle that felt uncomfortably familiar.

But it wasn't just the battle. I saw flashes of a lab, stark and sterile. People in white coats jabbing needles into my arm, vials of blood being taken away. I remembered pain, a searing, mind-numbing pain as something was injected into my system. And I remembered fear. A fear not of dying, but of what I was becoming.

I woke up to find Rain and Thunder watching me, a look of concern etched in their eyes. I reassured them with a weak smile, my mind still reeling from the intensity of the dreams. Could they really be memories? If so, they were fragments of a past life I didn't remember living.

Could it be possible that I was once a human, a soldier turned test subject in some clandestine experiment? Was my current state the result of some sort of failed experiment, a serum or a virus gone wrong? The more I pondered, the more questions I had, each one making my head throb in protest.

In this new world, I've learned that the past is irrelevant. What I was, who I was, doesn't change the reality of what I am now. But these dreams, these potential memories, feel important. They carry a weight that tugs at the edges of my consciousness. It's as if my past self is trying to tell me something, something crucial.

I don't know what it all means, and I'm not sure I want to. All I know is, I am what I am. A soldier, a test subject, a monster, a protector. Perhaps there's a reason I've become what I am now, and perhaps that reason lies within me, in my blood. Only time will tell. But until then, I must continue my journey, follow the trail and find the girl.

For in this shattered world, the past is but a shadow, and the future is all we've got left.

OCTOBER 19, YEAR UNKNOWN

The day began with the usual morning ritual of checking our surroundings, making sure the night hadn't brought anything uninvited to our doorstep. Thunder seemed more spirited today, as if the previous day's resting had given him renewed energy. Rain, the ever vigilant companion, was the first to sniff the air and point towards the west.

We'd picked up the girl's scent again. It was faint, almost elusive, but undoubtedly there. A peculiar mix of fear, desperation, and a faint whiff of her lingering essence. I could sense Rain's excitement, her tail wagging faster than usual. Thunder, too, seemed to sense our purpose and stood tall, his fiery eyes gleaming with anticipation.

We set out at a brisk pace, following the girl's scent, each of us tuned into our respective roles. Rain took the lead, her nose sniffing the air and ground, picking up and following the girl's trail. Thunder, with his superior strength and speed, served as our protector, his heightened senses alert to any potential danger. And I...I was the heart of the team, the one who gave direction and made the decisions.

As we ventured further into the wilderness, the day wore on, the sun slowly sinking towards the horizon. We didn't come across any other beings, human or otherwise. It was just us, and the endless expanse of the world left behind.

Every so often, I'd catch myself wondering about the girl. What made her run? Why leave the doll behind? And why was she so important to me? Was it just guilt? Or did her presence stir some deeply buried human emotion in me?

As night began to fall, we decided to set up camp. Rain snuggled close to me, her body providing a source of warmth in the chill of the night. Thunder took his place a few steps away, his glowing eyes scanning the surroundings, a silent sentinel in the dark.

And as I sat there, under the starlit sky, with the scent of the girl still fresh in our minds, I couldn't help but feel a strange sense of hope. Hope that we'd find her, hope that she'd be okay, and hope that maybe, just maybe, we were not as alone as we thought.

OCTOBER 20, YEAR UNKNOWN

A full moon hung in the sky, casting long, strange shadows on the ground as we settled into camp for the night. Thunder, whose fiery gaze never seemed to wane, had assumed his watchful position on the perimeter. Rain was curled up beside me, her warm body a comforting presence. But comfort was a fleeting sensation in this world.

The eeriness of the night had just started to seep into my consciousness when Rain's ears perked up. A low growl rumbled from her throat, a stark warning in the silence. Thunder's stance shifted, alert and poised for action.

The scent came first, a noxious blend of rot and decay, tainted with something terrifyingly familiar. Then, the rustling sounds, circling our camp, like whispers in the wind. Our camp was surrounded. But by what?

I didn't need the light of the moon to see them as they emerged from the shadows - a pack of hulking figures, their eyes glowing in the dark. Wolves. Their once majestic forms now distorted, reduced to skeletal structures, ravaged by the hunger and the virus that plagued them. Zombie wolves, each one a gruesome testament to the world that had been.

I felt a chill creep down my spine as I took in the situation. We were trapped. There was no way to outrun them; the wolves were too fast, too many. Thunder reared up, a chilling sight in the moonlight, his eyes aflame with defiance. Rain's growl grew louder, her body tensed and ready to fight.

I took a deep, steadying breath, feeling the cold air fill my lungs. If it was a fight they wanted, it was a fight they would get. I wasn't about to let this camp be taken over by a pack of wolves, zombie or not.

We were survivors, each in our own way. We had fought and bled, lost and won. And tonight, under the gaze of the full moon, we would prove once again why we were the last ones standing.

OCTOBER 21, YEAR UNKNOWN

Yesterday's wolf encounter was a horrifying reminder of our constant danger. I'd thought being trapped in the middle of a zombie wolf pack would be our end. But it seems every experience we've had, every struggle, every pain, was a lesson meant to prepare us for moments like these.

I remembered the fumes from the fuel at the service station and how it had incapacitated me. Could it work on the wolves, too? It was a desperate thought, a half-baked plan, but desperation is a powerful motivator.

After rooting through our supplies, I found a small container of ethyl ether in the first aid kit. A powerful anaesthetic in the old world, now, maybe a savior in this one. I saturated a cloth with the liquid, the sharp, potent smell making my eyes water. As the wolves closed in, snarling and baring their decaying teeth, I threw the cloth towards them.

The effect was immediate and staggering. The wolves recoiled, their keen senses overwhelmed by the harsh chemical. A chaotic chorus of whimpering and howling erupted as they staggered away, disoriented.

In that instant, we broke camp. Thunder, Rain and I bolted away from the scene, pushing our bodies to their limits. The disoriented howling of the wolves became a distant echo as we put as much distance between us and them as possible.

As the adrenaline of the escape wore off and a new day dawned, a mixed sense of relief and dread washed over me. We had escaped a dangerous encounter, but who knew what awaited us in this unpredictable, perilous world? For now, we continued, a peculiar trio united by survival in a world that seemed determined to tear us apart.

We are survivors. And today, we survived again.

OCTOBER 22, YEAR UNKNOWN

Today's trek led us to an unexpected sight, a sight both horrifying and grotesquely fascinating - a grocery store from the old world that had been transformed into a macabre butcher shop. Human carcasses were strewn across the street, an unfathomable reminder of the depravity humans were capable of when survival became the only law. The occupants of this gruesome outpost were three human survivors. The girl was there, inside.

As we approached, Rain growled low in her throat, hackles raised. Thunder whinnied and stamped his hooves nervously. They sensed the danger before we even saw it. I felt a shiver run through my undead body, not of cold, but of anticipation. I had to tread carefully.

Through a gap in the barricade, I watched the three survivors. They were ragged and gaunt, hardened by the trials they had endured. They were survivors, just like us, but their survival came at a cost that was clear in the horrifying display outside their sanctuary.

The girl was there, looking smaller and more vulnerable than ever. She didn't notice us yet, her focus entirely on the floor beneath her feet, possibly avoiding the gazes of her captors.

I felt an unfamiliar surge of protective anger swell within me. She was in danger, and I had brought this upon her. I had let her go. This was my responsibility. The spark of humanity I had felt before was now a raging fire. A zombie, a dog, a horse, we had become an unlikely family, and we weren't leaving anyone behind. Tonight, we needed a plan, a way to get her out safely. We had survived thus far; we had to keep surviving, keep fighting.

Tonight, I feel more alive than I have in a long, long time. It's ironic, really. I'm dead but never have I felt more purpose, more drive, more human. I guess in this world of the dead, it's these moments, these choices, that define who we truly are. And tonight, we are not just survivors. We are rescuers. We are family.

OCTOBER 23, YEAR UNKNOWN

As the dawn broke, we laid out our plans. We were going to use Thunder as our battering ram. He was strong, he was quick, he was frightening. The perfect diversion. He also, it seemed, harbored a deep dislike for the humans in that grocery store. When I told him about our plan, I swear I saw an understanding flicker in his dead eyes.

We charged at the grocery store, Thunder leading the onslaught. The impact shattered the makeshift barricade, splintering wood and sending debris flying in all directions. We stormed in, a one-zombie cavalry. I've never felt power like that before, the rush of adrenaline, the thrill of danger. My humanity was a shield, protecting me from the gruesome scene that awaited me inside.

The men were taken aback by our entrance. Before they could even comprehend what was happening, I had dealt with them. I didn't kill them. No, that would have been a mercy. I left them incapacitated, injured, in the horror of their own creation.

She was there, huddled in the corner. Her eyes were wide and frightened, her body trembling. She'd been force-fed to fatten her up, a horrifying realization that turned my stomach. But she was alive. She was safe.

I swept her up into my arms, and she clung onto me tightly, her sobs filling the air. She didn't stop crying. I couldn't blame her. What she had endured, what she had seen, was unimaginable. But she was alive, and now, she was safe.

We rode away from that place, leaving behind the terror and the horror. We rode into the sunrise, the soft glow of the morning light providing a stark contrast to the darkness we'd just left behind.

She clung to me tightly, her sobs subsiding gradually, replaced by quiet sniffling. I could feel her fear, her relief, her grief. I held her tighter, offering what little comfort I could. She'd survived hell, and she'd come out stronger. She was a survivor, just like us. We were a family, a strange, mismatched family in a world gone mad. But in that moment, as the first rays of the sun kissed our faces, we were invincible.

OCTOBER 24, YEAR UNKNOWN

Today was a quiet day, a day of rest. After the horror and exertion of yesterday, we needed it. The girl, especially, needed it. She had been through too much, experienced too much. Today, she needed peace.

We found a place to camp for the day, a secluded spot by a creek. The sound of running water was soothing, a peaceful lullaby in the otherwise oppressive silence. There was even a small patch of greenery, a small oasis amidst the devastation. It wasn't much, but it was enough.

The girl, whom I've come to think of as 'Silence', spent most of the day sleeping. She clung to her old, broken doll as if it were a lifeline, her fingers curled tightly around its tiny, worn-out body. Rain stayed by her side, a faithful guardian, offering her warmth and protection. It was a heartwarming sight, the dog and the girl, two innocent beings caught up in this cruel world, finding solace in each other.

I spent the day tending to Thunder and working on minor tasks, like mending a tear in my jacket or sharpening the blade of my knife. I also spent a fair bit of time just watching Silence and Rain, their peaceful rest a stark contrast to the harrowing events of yesterday.

In the quiet moments, in the silence punctuated only by the soft murmuring of the creek and the occasional soft whine from Rain, I allowed my mind to wander. I thought about our journey so far, about the horrors we had seen and the triumphs we had experienced. I thought about our purpose, our goal, our mission.

In the end, as the sun dipped below the horizon, painting the sky in hues of orange and purple, I came to one conclusion. Our mission, our goal, wasn't just to survive. It was to live. To truly live, despite the darkness that surrounded us. And today, as we took a moment to rest, to heal, to just be, we were doing exactly that. We were living.

Tonight, as Silence sleeps soundly next to a watchful Rain, and Thunder rests nearby, I find myself filled with a strange sense of contentment. Despite the chaos, despite the madness, we've found a moment of peace. A moment of respite. A moment to just live. And for now, that is enough.

OCTOBER 25, YEAR UNKNOWN

There is an apprehension in my chest as I wake up this morning, a knot of uncertainty that I can't shake off. For the first time since this strange journey began, I am not worried about our survival, or about the dangers that lie ahead. No, today, my fear is of a different nature.

Today, I am scared of rejection, of the potential backlash that my attempt at communication might incite. Silence, the young woman we rescued, has started to recover. Her eyes have lost that glazed, faraway look, replaced instead with a cautious alertness. She's been quiet, hardly leaving Rain's side, but I can see the strength in her, a resiliency that is both admirable and heart-rending.

For a while now, I have been wondering about the word 'baby', the one she had scrawled on the mirror back at the motel. It's been gnawing at me, a puzzle that refuses to be solved. And today, I finally muster the courage to confront it.

It is mid-morning when I approach her, my hands trembling slightly, my throat dry. The apprehension is a palpable thing, a heavy cloak around my shoulders. With every step towards her, my heart beats a wild rhythm in my chest.

But when I finally reach her, when I finally manage to croak out the word 'baby', her reaction is not what I expect. There is no fear in her eyes, no rejection or hatred. Instead, she just looks at me, her eyes large and full of a quiet understanding. And then, she does something that takes me by surprise.

She reaches out, her small hand gripping my larger one, and she pulls me towards her. For a moment, I am frozen in place, shocked by the unexpected gesture. But then, slowly, hesitantly, I allow myself to be pulled in, to be held close by this small, fragile human.

We stay like that for what feels like hours, Silence and me, our silent communication more profound than any words could ever be. And as I sit there, with her small hand in mine and her body pressed against mine, I feel something break inside me, a wall that I hadn't known existed.

I don't know what this means for our journey, for our mission. But for now, I feel a strange sense of relief, of unburdening. And as we sit there, in the quiet of the morning, I feel, for the first time in a very long time, a glimmer of hope.

OCTOBER 26, YEAR UNKNOWN

This morning, an interesting development took place. After days of apprehension and silence, our young companion, Silence, finally seems to have found a reason to break out of her shell. And that reason, surprisingly enough, is Thunder.

I woke to the curious sound of laughter, a sweet, clear melody that I hadn't heard in so long that it felt foreign to my ears. As I roused myself and peered out of our makeshift shelter, the sight that greeted me was one I'll carry in my mind forever.

There was Silence, her hair billowing around her as she sat atop Thunder, her hands clutching his coarse mane, her face a picture of pure joy. Thunder, in his own way, seemed to be basking in her attention, his large eyes fixed on the young girl with a softness that belied his monstrous form.

For a moment, I watched, my heart aching with a mixture of happiness and sorrow. Happiness for the laughter that echoed in our camp, the bond forming between the girl and the zombie horse. Sorrow for the world that once was, for the innocence that was lost, for the normal childhood that Silence had been robbed of.

Throughout the day, Silence spent most of her time with Thunder, exploring the boundaries of their new friendship. She would clamber onto his back, her small body almost disappearing into his vastness, and they would roam around the area, her gentle laughter trailing behind them.

By evening, when we huddled around our small fire, Silence was exhausted, but content. She fell asleep with her head resting against Thunder's flank, his soft, rhythmic breaths lulling her to sleep. As I watched them, my heart heavy in my chest, I was reminded of how incredibly resilient life can be, of how even amidst chaos and devastation, bonds can form, and hope can flourish.

It's strange how this journey has changed me. I am not just a creature of survival anymore. I am a witness to the enduring spirit of life, to the strength of bonds formed in adversity. I am a caretaker, a companion, and, in some strange way, a friend. And as the fire flickers in the darkness, casting long shadows over our camp, I am filled with a sense of determination.

Tomorrow, we continue our journey, and I am more resolved than ever to see it through, to find the place that the film reel hinted at, for Silence, for Rain, for Thunder, and for me.

OCTOBER 27, YEAR UNKNOWN

The road ahead has been cut off by a landslide, forcing us to face an alternate route that chills me to the bone - a long-abandoned mine shaft cutting through the mountain. As we pack our meager belongings and mount Thunder, a dark opening in a nearby mountain stands menacingly against the morning glow. It is a mine shaft, its mouth gaping ominously, beckoning us into its inky depths. I cannot see what lies beyond, but I can feel it, a chilling wind whispering stories of the past, of desperate miners, and now of a potential pathway to our future. Our path leads directly into it, and we have no choice but to delve deep into the heart of the mountain.

As we stand before the entrance, I can see the trepidation in Silence's eyes, mirrored in Rain's quiet whine. Thunder too, senses the palpable unease, his massive form shifting restlessly beneath me. I feel an odd sensation; a strange sense of familiarity creeps over me. The realization hits with the subtlety of a brick; this mine, this abandoned slice of man's subterranean meddling, I've been here before. I remember the echoes of picks and shovels, and of men's laughter, from a different life, a different me. The thought unnerves me, leaving a sour taste of apprehension in my mouth... if you can call it that. I shake it off, focusing on the task at hand. We are about to venture into the bowels of the earth. The girl seems to sense my unease, her small hand reaching out to clutch mine in a shared moment of uncertainty. The darkness yawns before us, swallowing all light, an impenetrable veil that forces a shiver down my spine.

To enter is madness. To proceed is necessity.

So, we venture forth. The light from a makeshift torch dances erratically on the rough hewn stone walls, the only source of illumination in this endless abyss. The echoes of our footsteps are the only sound breaking the deafening silence, a reminder of our alien presence in this forsaken place.

The chill in the air is more than just temperature. It is a foreboding, a warning of the darkness that lies ahead. We journey further in, the darkness closing around us, a haunting symphony of whispers and echoes our only company.

Halfway through the tunnel, a sudden collapse almost separates us. A shower of dirt and rock plummets from the ceiling, causing us to scatter in panic. Dust clouds our vision, choking us, and for a moment, the world is nothing but noise and confusion. When it finally settles, Silence is on the other side of the rubble, separated from us. She's scared but unhurt. It takes hours of careful work, but we manage to clear a path and reunite.

As we emerge from the other side of the tunnel, it feels as if we've been reborn. The light of the setting sun is a welcome sight after the oppressive darkness, the fresh air a sweet relief against the stale confines of the mine. Our journey through the mountain is over. We are shaken, but undeterred.

This ordeal is yet another testament to our resilience. In the face of darkness, we held onto hope. We've come out stronger, our bonds reinforced in the crucible of shared fear and triumph. Tonight, as we settle down under the twinkling stars, their light seems a bit brighter, the silence a bit more comforting. Today, we stared into the abyss, and came out the other side. What else can stand in our way?

Tomorrow, we press on. For now, we rest.

OCTOBER 28, YEAR UNKNOWN

Today, we had a close encounter with modern technology that's somehow survived the apocalypse - a drone. As we stumbled down a mountain slope, squinting in the bright daylight, the mechanical hum of a drone filled the air. These things were always a nuisance in the old world, a pesky interruption of peace. Now, they've become much more sinister.

Thunder, the girl, and I had to dive for cover, our bodies pressed against the uneven, rocky ground. We were fortunate to be near a copse of dead trees. Their skeletal remains provided us with a shield from the prying eyes in the sky. I could sense Thunder's unease, his large eyes rolling nervously, and I did my best to soothe him. I felt the girl grip onto my arm tightly, her small frame shaking beside me.

For what felt like an eternity, we lay there, hidden and holding our breath as the drone hovered overhead, its relentless buzzing echoing through the silent landscape. Then, finally, the sound receded into the distance, leaving us in quiet once again.

We wasted no time getting back on Thunder and putting some distance between us and the drone's last known location. As we traveled further, I couldn't help but worry about who - or what - was controlling that drone. There's a faceless enemy out there, somewhere, using these machines to scour the land for... what? Survivors? Resources? Or something else? This world's dangers are not just the mindless undead, but also these unseen threats. We need to remain vigilant. Tomorrow, we push on.

OCTOBER 29, YEAR UNKNOWN

Today was a day of incessant rain, a wet reminder of the world we once knew. It fell in sheets, drenching the land, Thunder, the girl, and myself. The sky was an unending slate gray, the wind carrying the cold touch of moisture. Thunder plodded on through the muddy ground, while we huddled under the remnants of a tarp I had scavenged days ago.

There's a kind of beauty in the rain, I suppose. It's one of the few things left that's not a grotesque caricature of the past. It feels... normal. But it also brings complications. It chills to the bone, making movement sluggish and stiff. It dampens the sound, masking possible threats.

The girl seemed to find some comfort in the downpour, letting the rain wash over her. Maybe it cleansed her of the horrors she'd witnessed, however briefly. I watched her extend a hand out from our shelter, letting the droplets fall onto her palm. She'd draw patterns on the wet ground, her movements careful, almost reverent. It was a moment of peace in our unending turmoil.

But even the rain couldn't wash away our fears. The drone encounter still fresh in our minds, I spent the day on high alert, my eyes scanning the gloomy landscape for any signs of movement. For now, it seems we are safe. But in this world, safety is a fleeting concept. Tomorrow, we press on, come rain or shine.

OCTOBER 30, YEAR UNKNOWN

Today we stumbled upon a town - a forgotten relic of a world that no longer exists. It was quiet and empty, the life that once thrived there now just echoes in the emptiness. We approached it with caution, fearful of unseen dangers, but there was no one and nothing to threaten us.

As we moved deeper into the town, the silent streets gave way to an unexpected sight - a fairground. It stood there, untouched by the mayhem of the apocalypse. The Ferris wheel towered over the surrounding buildings, its cars empty and immobile. The merry-go-round stood silent, its once vibrant colors faded, the music silenced forever.

I can only imagine the sights and sounds that once filled this place. The laughter of children, the cheerful music, the clatter of roller coaster cars, and the screams of joy and fright as they plunged down the steep tracks. All those human experiences, those precious moments of life, they seem alien to me now.

The girl got off Thunder and tentatively approached the merry-go-round. She ran her fingers over the faded paint of a carousel horse. For the first time since we found her, a small smile crept onto her face. It was as if this place, a symbol of joy and life, could touch something inside her, despite everything she had been through.

I found an old generator and managed to get it running. As night fell, the lights of the fairground flickered to life, casting a soft glow over the abandoned town. It felt like we had brought a small piece of the past back to life, even if it was just for a night.

For a brief moment, we were not lost souls in a post-apocalyptic world. We were just beings, living a quiet moment in an illuminated bubble of the past. The fairground, the girl's smile, the gentle glow of the lights - it felt like a respite from our grim reality.

Tomorrow we'll move on, but tonight we sleep under the glow of the Ferris wheel, with the silence of the fairground as our lullaby.

OCTOBER 31, YEAR UNKNOWN

Today, it all came to a head. The shadows we thought were following us from a distance came right up to our doorstep, gnashing their teeth and salivating with a hunger that mirrored my own from days ago. They were the zombie wolves that we had managed to avoid until now.

Thunder, the warrior he was born to be, lunged into action before I could even comprehend what was happening. He rammed into the first few wolves, killing them on the spot. His zombie strength was brutal, deadly and unfortunately, not enough.

I saw it happen in slow motion. Silence, my quiet, frightened little friend, was almost a goner. A wolf lunged at her. Rain, my ever-faithful companion, jumped in between at the last second, taking the bite for her. The resulting scream that filled the air was a sound I will never forget. Rain howled, a pained, terrified sound, as they both tumbled away from the girl.

Seeing Rain hurt, seeing the terror in Silence's eyes, something in me snapped. I felt a surge of power, a primal instinct taking over. I fought. I fought like I've never fought before. I was a beast. I was a monster. I was a zombie.

My hands met fur and flesh and bones, rending and tearing with a force that scared me. The wolves didn't stand a chance. In the end, they were nothing but bodies strewn across the ground, victims of the monster that I am. The monster that I've been trying to hide from.

Silence is safe now. She's scared, but unharmed. Rain, I don't know where she is. I can only hope she will come back to us. And as for me, I am utterly drained. But I am reminded once again, in the most brutal way possible - I am the last zombie.

NOVEMBER 1, YEAR UNKNOWN

sLeep

NOVEMBER 2, YEAR UNKNOWN

The world has a way of forcing you to confront the harsh truths about yourself. Yesterday was one such day. I spent today in a daze, remembering the ferocious beast I had become. But if there's one thing I've learned, it's that dwelling on the past won't get us anywhere. We need to move forward. For Silence's sake, for Rain's sake, for my own.

I woke up late today, my body still sore and weary from the fight. Silence was sitting a few feet away, her back to me, hugging her knees to her chest. There was a profound sadness about her, a quiet acceptance of our harsh reality. I found myself wishing I could do something to ease her pain, to reassure her that we would be okay. But words elude me and even if they didn't, I doubt she would understand. I'm a monster, after all.

I spent most of the day scavenging the area. It was strange, being in a ghost town. A place that was once bustling with life was now nothing but a graveyard of broken dreams and forgotten lives. I found some canned food and a couple of blankets. Not much, but it would suffice.

Rain is still missing. Every rustle of leaves, every whisper of wind, I find myself hoping it's her. I've never felt so helpless before. I want to go out there, to search for her, to bring her back. But there's Silence to think about. I can't leave her alone. I can only hope that Rain makes her way back to us.

Tonight, we will sleep under the starless sky, huddled against the cold. Thunder, somehow untouched by the mayhem, was the calm in the storm, standing a vigilant watch over our fitful rest. We are survivors, Silence and I. We are both fighters. We will not give up. Not now, not ever. I need to keep telling myself that. I need to believe in it. Because if I don't, if I let the despair take over, then we truly are lost.

And so, we carry on. In this bleak and desolate world, we carry on.

NOVEMBER 3, YEAR UNKNOWN

The rain hasn't let up, relentless in its pursuit. It's almost a metaphor for our journey, unending, cold, and unforgiving. Rain, my loyal companion, is back. But he's different. He maintains a distance, far out of reach, and there is a wild look in his eyes. The same look the wolves had.

He's been bitten. I had hoped the change wouldn't affect him like this, but here we are. He's a familiar shadow that haunts the corner of my vision. His gaze lingers on Silence for moments too long, and it chills me to the bone. I need to find a way to reverse this, to bring Rain back to us.

The rest of the day is a blur, all of us marching on against the elements, against the world. We find an abandoned barn and seek shelter from the storm. The comfort of the dry straw bed is lost on me, my thoughts preoccupied with Rain. The little girl clings onto the ragged doll, now a silent token of her painful past. Thunder stands guard outside, a silent sentinel against the hostile world.

I've seen what this virus can do, what it has done to me. But the fear for Rain, it's different, it's more personal. He's not just a dog. He's family, my family. And as I drift off to a restless sleep, the haunting echo of his mournful howl is the only sound that pierces the incessant drumming of the rain on the barn's rusty roof.

NOVEMBER 4, YEAR UNKNOWN

I should be more careful. But seeing Rain like this, different but alive, has shaken me. I wish I could comfort him, let him know it's okay, we're still the same, we can still be friends. But he's keeping his distance. Maybe he's as scared of me as I am of him. And, I can't blame him. I'd be scared too, of a creature like me.

The rain continues. I look at Silence. She's holding on, brave in her silence. She's endured so much, seen things no one should ever have to see, especially not a child. I owe it to her to keep moving. We owe it to each other. We're all we've got.

Thunder's been a rock, unflinching in his duty, unfaltering in his stride. And now with Rain... changed, he's been more watchful than ever. We'll find a way to make it work. We have to. We've come too far to let the fear of the unknown stop us.

NOVEMBER 5, YEAR UNKNOWN

Silence spent a lot of time today with her doll. She was unusually persistent, making attempts to communicate. She pointed at the doll, then at her belly, then back at the doll again. It was heart-wrenching to see her struggle with words, her voice a distant memory.

Baby... She's trying to say baby. The realisation hit me like a punch in the gut. It all makes sense now. Her doll, her desperate attempts to communicate, her sudden departure from our side before. She's been trying to tell us about a baby. Her baby.

Is it still alive? Is that why she left us before? To go back for her baby? And we... I, was too slow to understand. How could I have missed it? But then again, who could imagine such a responsibility resting on such tiny shoulders.

I find my eyes stinging. I don't know if zombies can cry, but right now, I feel like I might. We need to find her baby. I look at Silence, her face illuminated by the flickering fire, her eyes haunted but determined. We'll find your baby, Silence. I promise.

NOVEMBER 6, YEAR UNKNOWN

Racked my brains all night and most of today for any leads on where Silence's baby could be. The lack of clear communication is frustrating, but we're working with what we have. Silence, for her part, is patient and as clear as she can be. She points in a general direction often - North.

We came across a small building today - an old church, dilapidated and mostly overtaken by wild vegetation. It stood alone, almost solemn in its isolation, and despite my initial apprehension, we decided to take a look. There was something about it that pulled me in.

Inside, we found a map, a detailed map of the area. It's old and frayed at the edges, but still usable. The North had a cluster of buildings drawn together, marked in faded ink - looks like a settlement or community of some sort. I don't know if it means anything, but it's the only clue we have for now.

Tonight, under the shadow of the old church, we prepare to sleep. Thunder's hooves echo softly in the silence as he grazes nearby, while Rain watches us from a distance, her eyes glinting in the dark.

North. We go North tomorrow.

NOVEMBER 7, YEAR UNKNOWN

Had vivid dreams last night. Dreams that felt real, more real than anything in this post-apocalyptic existence. I saw faces, familiar ones, even though I can't place them in my waking life. I saw myself, not as the creature I am now, but as a man.

There were images of labs, cold and sterile, filled with monitors and medical equipment. The hum of machinery filled my ears. Men and women in white lab coats. Procedures, injections, all in a haze. I saw a symbol, an insignia, maybe of an organization or institution.

One face stood out, a man, older, with gray hair and sharp eyes. He wore glasses and a stern expression. He seemed important, like he held answers. His face is etched clearly in my mind, as if inviting me to remember.

I woke up with a start, my mind filled with fragmented memories. I don't know what these dreams mean, but there is a sense of urgency now. We need to find that community on the map. I need answers.

Today, we push North. I feel it in my bones, that we are getting closer, that the dreams are leading us somewhere. I have no idea what awaits us, but we have to keep moving.

Silence has been quiet today, more than usual, lost in her own thoughts. Rain is still aloof, yet she follows at a distance, a ghostly guardian of sorts. And Thunder, well, Thunder is just happy to be on the move.

Tonight, under the vast, starry sky, we rest. We're a motley crew, driven by a purpose none of us fully understand. But we press on, under the guidance of half-remembered dreams and silent hopes.

NOVEMBER 8, YEAR UNKNOWN

It happened so quickly. One minute, it was peaceful; the next, we were surrounded. A rumble in the distance, a cloud of dust on the horizon, and then they were upon us. Military vehicles, a convoy, with armed soldiers spilling out, spreading like an infestation. They had a wild look in their eyes, driven by desperation, or perhaps the madness this world has come to know too well.

Silence was quicker, even in her condition. She darted into the underbrush, Thunder in tow. They disappeared into the thick foliage before I could even react. I caught sight of them just long enough to see that they were safe, out of the immediate danger zone.

Then it was just Rain and me. She growled, her hackles raised, a primal warning that went unheeded. As they got closer, we had no choice but to run. We had to lead them away from Silence and Thunder.

We went west, Rain leading the way. I did my best to keep up, each breath burning my lungs, the world a dizzying blur of movement. We cut through the trees, jumped over obstacles, and dashed through shallow streams, anything to shake them off our trail.

As the hours passed, we lost sight of them. But the sounds of the vehicles still echoed in the distance, a chilling reminder of the danger we had narrowly escaped.

I don't know how far we ran or where we are now. All I know is that we are lost, separated from Silence and Thunder. As the sky began to darken, I decided we should rest. We'll need all the strength we can muster to reunite with them tomorrow.

The worry gnaws at me. Are they okay? Will we find them? For the first time in a long time, I find myself wishing for the clarity of my past self, for a plan, for anything but the uncertainty that gnaws at my gut.

Tonight, we sleep under a canopy of unfamiliar stars, accompanied only by the howling of Rain and the cold dread of the unknown. Tomorrow, we find them, or we die trying.

NOVEMBER 9, YEAR UNKNOWN

Rain approached me today. That's a first since her transformation. She was edgy, always looking toward the direction we'd left Silence and Thunder, but she came to me. No aggression. No immediate threat. Just a quiet kind of curiosity. Or perhaps resignation. I can't be sure. I offered her a hand, but she kept a safe distance.

We have been traveling through desolate fields and forests, sticking to the low ground to stay hidden from prying eyes. Both of us are silent, as if a spoken word would shatter the tenuous peace we've managed to carve out in this fractured world.

I wonder if she remembers. If she knows who she used to be, or if her transformation has robbed her of those memories. For myself, I can remember my past life, the man I used to be. But the specifics... they're more like wisps of cloud, tantalizingly close, but gone when I try to grasp them.

By midday, we reach an old barn, dilapidated but standing. A suitable shelter to take a rest. Rain seems uneasy, restless. She's sniffing the air with unease. I decide to climb the hayloft for a better look around. But what I find leaves me stunned.

I recognize this place, or somewhere like it. The barn, the fields around. A sense of dread washes over me. This place... This is where it started. My journey into the unknown, into the hell that's my existence now. It was here that I was changed. But why? How? The answers elude me.

Rain's growl brings me back to the present. It's time to move on. We have to regroup with Silence and Thunder. And hopefully, avoid the military.

But this barn... I can't shake the feeling. It's a piece of my lost past. And possibly a key to our future.

NOVEMBER 10, YEAR UNKNOWN

I woke up with Rain's jaws inches from my face. Her eyes were glassy, as if not entirely present. I held still, a survival instinct keeping my pulse steady. Her teeth were bare, a low growl emanating from her throat.

Then, like a bolt of lightning, she lunged. I rolled away in the nick of time, but not without feeling the brush of her fangs against my skin. She snapped again, and I kicked her off me. She yelped, skidding away on the dusty barn floor.

It was my turn to growl. I could feel the anger bubbling, the red haze starting to cloud my vision. But I fought it back. It wouldn't do us any good to be at each other's throats.

Rain was just as shaken. She was pacing now, eyes wild and ears flat against her skull. It was almost as if she was fighting some internal battle of her own. As if she didn't want to hurt me but couldn't fight the compulsion to do so.

I gave her space, letting her sort out whatever was going on in her head. Meanwhile, I busied myself with checking my gear, my thoughts spiraling. We needed to find Silence and Thunder. And we needed to do it fast.

By the time I was ready to leave, Rain had calmed down. She kept her distance, but there was a new kind of understanding between us. As if we'd crossed some invisible line.

We left the barn behind, the memory of my past and our near clash, and trudged on. The weight of our predicament sat heavy on my shoulders. But one thing was clear. We were in this together. And together, we'd have to face whatever comes our way.

NOVEMBER 11, YEAR UNKNOWN

The sky was still a gunmetal gray when we reached the river. It was a torrent now, swollen with the relentless rain that had been hammering down for hours. It rushed past in a loud, unyielding current that turned my stomach. How were we supposed to cross this?

Rain stayed back, watching me warily as I surveyed the situation. She was afraid, I could see it in her. The water would be cold, the current strong. There was no telling what waited beneath the surface. For a moment, I wished Thunder was here. His large, sturdy form would have been a comfort.

I spotted a fallen tree downstream, but it was too narrow, too slick with rain. Not to mention, it was precariously perched over the raging water. A single wrong move, and we'd be swept away. That wasn't a risk I was willing to take.

There was a bridge further up, but it was too exposed. A large, obvious crossing that would undoubtedly draw attention from any wandering eyes. Still, it might be our only option.

I turned to Rain, communicating with my eyes what my mouth couldn't. She seemed to understand, giving a low, affirmative bark. I hesitated, feeling the weight of the decision. Then, with a last look at the churning river, I led the way towards the bridge.

Every step felt heavy, weighed down by the uncertainty of what lay ahead. But we had no choice. We had to move forward, towards the unknown. For us, for Silence, for her missing child. As I set my foot on the damp, wooden planks of the bridge, I felt a strange mix of fear and determination. This was just another obstacle, another challenge. We would overcome this, just like we had everything else. Together.

NOVEMBER 12, YEAR UNKNOWN

The skies roared and the earth wept today. It's been a deluge since dawn. The rain is unrelenting, a harsh curtain of water drenching everything. Not a day for travelling. Thunder seems restless in this weather, as if the storm's chaos resonates with his unnatural form. As for Rain, she's distant, hesitant.

We found an abandoned barn to take shelter. It's half collapsed and barely offers any respite from the torrential downpour, but it's better than the open road. The wooden floor is soaked, the roof is leaking, and there's an unpleasant dampness to the air that seeps into your bones.

My thoughts keep drifting back to Silence. Alone out there, navigating through the storm. I worry for her, but I know she's smart, resourceful. I hope she found shelter, and I hope she's safe. I fear for her, yes, but not for the baby she constantly talks about. I wonder where that baby could be, out in this violent world.

I feel my own feral instincts growing, pushing at the edges of my consciousness. The storm, the separation, the concern... they're triggering something within me. I can't let it control me. I won't. I need to stay focused. Stay human.

It's going to be a long, wet night.

NOVEMBER 13, YEAR UNKNOWN

Rain has gone. I woke up this morning to a chill in the barn and an absence by my side. A swift survey confirmed it. Rain's not here. Her scent lingers, but it's fading fast. Rain's not in the vicinity. I called out, my voice barely audible over the rain, but there was no response.

Today's been a tough day, filled with frustration and fear. The worst of it? The loneliness. It's a hard, gnawing thing that tugs at your insides and reminds you of just how alone you really are. And it's made worse by the empty space where Rain used to be. Her absence is a void, a hollow, gaping wound that just seems to amplify the silence.

I hope she's safe. Wherever she is, whatever she's doing, I just hope she's safe. That's all I can do, really. Hope and wait.

Spent the rest of the day in the barn, pacing restlessly. The storm seems to have lost some of its fury, but it's still a dreary, sodden day.

My thoughts are a whirlpool, circling around Silence, around Rain, around the baby. I don't understand the compulsion to find them, to protect them. I don't understand this pull I feel towards them. I just know it's there. It's like a dull ache that won't go away, a nagging voice at the back of my head that refuses to be quieted.

Tomorrow, I'll try to find Rain's trail. If she's left one. And then... I don't know. The road's unclear, the way forward uncertain. But I can't just stay here. I need to do something.

And so, I wait for tomorrow. Another day. Another chance. Another hope.

NOVEMBER 14, YEAR UNKNOWN

I've never felt more alone. I woke up today, expecting to see Rain, forgetting for a moment that she wasn't there. The realization hit me like a physical blow, leaving me gasping for breath.

The loneliness is oppressive, suffocating, it pushes down on me, making it harder and harder to breathe. It's in these moments that I realize just how much I relied on Rain and Silence. I'm not just a zombie, I'm a lonely zombie. A lonely, helpless, pathetic creature with no one to turn to.

I don't know what triggered it, maybe it was the loneliness, the sense of helplessness, the fear, but something did. Suddenly, I was on the ground, my body shaking, my mind a whirlwind of images and thoughts, all jumbled and confused. It was like every memory, every emotion was fighting for dominance, leaving me in a state of utter chaos.

When it finally passed, I was left weak, spent. I lay there on the cold, damp ground, the world spinning around me, feeling more alone than ever. My mind was a mess, a tangled web of thoughts and emotions that I could barely comprehend.

I don't know how long I lay there, time seemed to lose all meaning. All I know is that when I finally managed to pull myself up, it was dark, the day had passed, and the world was quiet.

Tomorrow, I'll try again. I'll try to pick up Rain's trail, try to find Silence and the baby. Because that's all I can do. Try. Keep trying, keep pushing forward, no matter how hard it gets. Because the alternative... the alternative is too terrible to contemplate.

NOVEMBER 15, YEAR UNKNOWN

I walked right into it. Their makeshift camp. A handful of human survivors. They were as shocked to see me as I was to see them. They didn't run, didn't cower in fear. They attacked. I could have fought back, should have fought back. But I didn't.

They beat me. Clubs, fists, feet, anything they could find. I just took it, every blow, every kick. The pain was immense, but it was nothing compared to the pain inside. The pain of loss, of loneliness, of utter despair.

I didn't fight back. I just lay there, letting them vent their fear and hatred on me. I was their punching bag, their scapegoat, their outlet for all the frustration and anger and fear that this world has forced upon them. And for a while, I welcomed it. I welcomed the pain, the punishment. I felt like I deserved it.

And when they were done, when they'd spent all their rage and fear and frustration, they left me. Left me lying there in the dirt, broken and battered. I lay there, the pain a dull, throbbing ache, the loneliness a gaping, aching void.

But I didn't die. I couldn't die. Not yet. Not while there was still hope. Not while there was still a chance to find Silence and the baby. To find Rain.

I'm broken, beaten, but I'm not beaten. I will keep going. I will find them. I have to. For them. For me. For hope. For life.

NOVEMBER 16, YEAR UNKNOWN

Too tired to think

NOVEMBER 17, YEAR UNKNOWN

Sleep

NOVEMBER 18, YEAR UNKNOWN

I woke at sundown today. There's a kind of soothing tranquility in the dark that I find restorative. My broken arm throbs in time with my heartbeat, a steady, painful drum. I need to splint it, keep it steady to allow whatever semblance of healing I have left to work. But the work is a distraction, and I welcome it. The numbing ache in my mind, though, persists. A different kind of pain, unaided by any splint. It's a fog, a haze that veils the sharpness of the world.

I'd never thought I'd miss the clarity that pain brings, the harsh focus it provides, the living proof of my existence. Now, it's as if I'm floating, adrift in a sea of darkness. Thoughts seem to drift away as soon as they appear, slipping through my fingers like so many grains of sand. I need to find a way back, find my focus. For Silence, for Rain, for Thunder. They're relying on me.

Tomorrow, I'll set my arm. I'll bear the pain. And maybe, just maybe, I'll find a piece of myself along the way.

NOVEMBER 19, YEAR UNKNOWN

Today, I wrestled with my pain. I fashioned a crude splint out of sticks and some shredded fabric, then set to work. Straightening the bone... it hurt. Like nothing I've felt since the changes. It was raw, blinding agony. Every nerve screamed in protest, and the world seemed to spin and blur at the edges. I clenched my jaw, bit back a scream.

And then it was done. The arm felt heavy, awkward in the splint, but the bone was aligned. The gnawing pain subsided, became a dull throb. It was a success of sorts, a small triumph in the face of what felt like insurmountable odds.

That harsh bite of pain... it grounded me. Brought a moment of sharp, piercing clarity. I felt truly alive in that moment, in a way that's been elusive lately. It was a bitter reminder of what I once was, a taste of the human existence that I'd forgotten. The pain was awful, but also, strangely comforting. I existed. I was here, fighting, surviving.

Silence, Rain, Thunder... They're out there somewhere. They're counting on me. And I won't let them down. Tomorrow, I press on.

NOVEMBER 20, YEAR UNKNOWN

Water. My worst enemy, my harshest punishment. Today, it tried to claim me. The flooded river... it swallowed me whole. My mind was a fog, thick and stifling. Did I circle back to the same river, or was this a new swell? I couldn't tell, couldn't think.

The water was freezing, brutal in its indifference. It ripped at me, clawed at me, pulled me under. I struggled against it, my good arm reaching, grasping, holding onto the sharp, slippery rocks on the edge. My lungs burned. My eyes stung.

Rain appeared then, a blur of movement on the riverbank. She was snarling, baring her teeth. Was she attacking? Trying to help? I couldn't tell. Pain exploded in my arm. Was she pulling me to safety? I saw a flash of bone, blood, felt an agonizing tear. I lost my grip, got swept away. The last thing I saw was Rain on the bank, her vice grip shaking violently the limb and bloodied cloth in her jaws.

Darkness took over then, cold and inviting. I welcomed it.

I don't know how much time passed. I woke up coughing, gasping. My clothes were soaked, my body numb from the cold. Thunder stood over me, I almost imagined concern in his eyes. Silence was there too, her fingers deftly bandaging the raw, blackened mess of my arm. They'd pulled me from the water, saved my life. My splint and sleeve were gone. Torn to shreds by Rain. But my arm, at least, was still very much attached to me.

Today, I came face to face with death. But I'm still here. And I have them to thank for that. Tomorrow, we continue our journey... together.

NOVEMBER 21, YEAR UNKNOWN

I woke up in a dry place. Safe. Silence, Thunder, even Rain watching cautiously from the other side of the bank. I tried to move and pain shot through my arm. Pain? I feel pain now? Looking at my arm, with the splint gone, my limb was now swollen and throbbing with a deep ache. It took me a moment to remember the river, the dog, and the horrifying fear of losing my arm.

The dog is watching me closely, a strange mix of concern and distrust in her eyes. She saved me, was that right? Was it her intention to save me or was she just ripping at my injured arm, her new instincts taking over? If ever there was a creature that embodied loyalty, it was Rain. I never knew a creature could care so much, could be so devoted to their pack. Despite her zombie status, I believed she retained the inherent goodness that was part of her nature. It was as if her transformation had stripped her to her core, revealing only the purest traits. Rain had been my constant companion, always by my side through the toughest of times.

Silence is there too, watching both of us with wide, worried eyes. The girl is holding onto my other hand tightly, as if scared I would disappear again.

My mind is a whirl of confusion. Nothing makes sense. One moment I was crossing the river, the next... Questions swarm like a horde of flies, and I don't have the energy or the clarity to swat them away. Instead, I let myself drift back into a much-needed sleep.

NOVEMBER 22, YEAR UNKNOWN

Rain is still there, on the other side of the bank. She is watching us, but maintains her distance. The cautiousness, the mistrust, it's etched in her movements. She looks well though, surprisingly agile. Maybe being bitten had somehow changed her. I can't say for certain. I only know that we're alive because of her. And yet, something tells me it wasn't for me she did it. It was for Silence, I suspect.

My arm throbs with each heartbeat, a constant reminder of my mistake, my carelessness. Silence has been fussing around, tearing strips from her own clothes to replace my tattered bandages. I can't tell her how much it means to me, her kindness, her trust.

I try to sit up, pushing past the searing pain in my arm. Silence brings me water. I remember the times when I would not have needed such things, and then I remember the hunger. I force myself to drink, hoping it will help. And then I sleep, falling into a fitful slumber haunted by strange dreams of soldiers, labs, and needles.

The day ends with Rain still on the other side, her gaze never straying far from our camp. The night is full of sounds, but the one that haunts me the most is Rain's howl, echoing through the wilderness, filled with a lonely sorrow that cuts me to the bone.

NOVEMBER 23, YEAR UNKNOWN

Rain looks bad. Her usually alert stance is slack and there's a tiredness in her eyes that makes my heart clench. The strength that once flowed through her seems to have evaporated overnight. I think back to the wolf attack, the bite. My body, it... heals itself, but what of Rain? She's different now, that much is clear. Is her change... is it like mine? Or worse?

I watch her from across the river, the water a gaping chasm between us. She's in pain, that much is clear, and my thoughts are whirring. I need to get to her, help her. But the river... It's a menacing beast, deep and fast, the cold currents threatening to sweep away anyone foolish enough to try and cross.

Thunder is restless. He trots up and down the bank, his whinnies filled with worry. Silence watches from the shelter of our camp, her face tight with concern. She trusts me. She knows I will do something, whatever it takes, to help our friend.

I start gathering materials. Ropes, wood, whatever flotsam the river has gifted us with. I'm going to build a raft, a desperate plan, but the only one I have. It's going to be a long night. I only hope it's not too late.

NOVEMBER 24, YEAR UNKNOWN

The sky is dark, and the clouds unleash a merciless torrent. It is as if the world itself conspires against us. My raft, my fragile hope, gets ripped away by the wild currents, smashed against the rocks downstream. I barely have time to swear before I hear Silence gasp. I turn around and see Rain collapse.

Thunder reacts before I do. The horse, with a determination that stuns me, steps into the frigid, churning river. He looks back at me, a silent command. I can see it in his eyes - 'This is the only way. Get on.'

In that moment, I feel a surge of gratitude for this undead horse, for his strength and courage. I hesitate for just a second, thinking of the risks, the dangers, then realize I don't have a choice.

Swallowing my fear, I mount Thunder. The river roars in my ears, its icy spray piercing through me, but Thunder stands resolute. If there's any chance of saving Rain, it's with Thunder. This is it. We have to cross, now or never.

Rain, heavy rain, outside and inside. We are sheltered from the storm's wrath in a small, dilapidated hut back on our side of the river. Silence watches on, petrified, clutching my jacket.

Rain is in bad shape though. Panting, his belly distended. It takes me a while to understand. He's not unwell, not sick - he's pregnant. A litter is on the way. The realization brings a flood of emotions, relief mingling with new anxiety. I'd always assumed Rain was a boy, but it seems I was wrong. I think back on the times she kept her distance, and suddenly it makes sense - she was nesting, hiding her condition. I feel foolish for not realizing it sooner.

Her panting is labored, her belly swollen, she's close. I hurriedly rummage through a nearby allotment, only finding some rags, discarded clothes. No towels, but they'll have to do. I layer them, making a makeshift birthing bed as best I can.

Silence is here too, her wide eyes reflecting the fear and uncertainty of the situation. Her grip on my jacket tightens. The storm rages outside, a cacophony of noise and chaos, matching the turmoil within us.

I can only hope now. Hope that Rain will be okay. Hope that the pups will be healthy. Hope that the storm outside, and inside, will pass soon. The echoes of my hopes are drowned in the noise of the storm, lost in the darkness of the night. But still, I hope.

NOVEMBER 26, YEAR UNKNOWN

The storm has subsided, the rain turned into a drizzle, and the new day brought a sense of calm. As the morning light trickles in, I see them - Rain's pups, squirming, blind, but very much alive. A litter of four, each no bigger than my hand, each a testament to life persisting against the odds.

Rain herself is much calmer, her breathing steady. She watches her pups with a motherly affection, feeding them and cleaning them in turn. The difference in her is stark. Her eyes, once hollow, are now filled with a new light. Her aggression is gone. She looks healthier, stronger - not just physically, but also emotionally. It's like her infection is cured.

I sit back, letting the scene unfold before me, letting the realization sink in. As my eyes wander to my arm, bandaged but throbbing with a dull ache, it hits me - Rain chewed the bloody rags. The rags soaked in my blood.

The dream that had been haunting me, clearer now, pieces into place. I remember the laboratory, the experiments, the vials. I remember being a test subject. My blood... It has the antidote. The cure. The very essence of life flowing through my veins can quell the infection, can restore life to its normalcy.

But how to use it, to bring it forth? That, I still need to figure out. But today, we celebrate. Celebrate Rain's recovery, celebrate the arrival of new life, celebrate the glimmer of hope my revelation brings. Today, we have found something we thought we'd lost – hope.

NOVEMBER 27, YEAR UNKNOWN

The morning begins with the urgent need to find food. Rain needs to replenish her strength after the birthing ordeal, and the pups will soon be needing more sustenance than she alone can provide. Thunder and I set out to forage.

We scour the nearby area for any edible plants, roots, and berries. We also have to take into account that Rain's diet should now include more protein. Our search leads us to a stream where Thunder catches some fish. I remember how it used to be - before all of this - the tranquility of fishing in a stream. The moment is not lost on me. It's a glimmer of the past, a fleeting memory of a simpler time.

Back at the camp, Silence is where we left her, attentively watching over Rain and the pups. She's surprisingly calm, even relaxed. It's like she understands the importance of her role, the responsibility she's taken on herself.

It's an exhausting day, but a rewarding one. We manage to gather a decent amount of food and bring it back to our camp. Rain devours the fish hungrily, and Silence, too, seems to enjoy the fresh catch. As I watch them, I realize that we've become a makeshift family in this broken world. And in that moment, I am hit by a wave of unexpected gratitude. Despite everything, we're here, we're surviving, and we have each other.

NOVEMBER 28, YEAR UNKNOWN

As darkness fell, distant echoes of human voices and mechanical noises reached our ears, sending a chill down our spines. The world outside of our little sanctuary had found us, and it was time to move again. We hastily gathered what we could, not daring to light a fire, as it would have drawn unwanted attention.

Silence wrapped the puppies in some of the fabric we found and secured them in a makeshift sling around her body. The sight was heart-wrenching; a child forced to shoulder responsibility far beyond her years, yet doing so with determination. Rain was still weak but managed to stay on her feet, nudging Silence reassuringly every now and then.

Thunder was anxious, pacing around us. His heightened senses were invaluable in these times. He was our alarm, our scout, our protector.

I watched them, my motley family, as we slipped away under the cover of night, leaving behind the closest thing we had to a home in a long time. It was a sad moment, but also a necessary one. Safety first, always.

In the midst of our escape, I managed to pen down these events of the day, my fingers stiff with cold, my heart heavy with the weight of the situation. The reality of our existence is harsh, yet we continue to push forward, together.

NOVEMBER 29, YEAR UNKNOWN

Today was a day of rest, something we all desperately needed after the past week's ordeal. We found a derelict barn, dry and just secluded enough to stay hidden. I noted a sense of security on everyone's face, at least for the moment. A sense of normalcy in a world gone mad.

Silence proved to be a brave and resourceful girl. She helped me create a new splint for my arm. We found some rusted iron rods and bandages in an old first aid kit that someone had left behind. She showed incredible resolve, as the sight of the grotesque swelling in my arm didn't seem to faze her. She treated the task like a puzzle that needed to be solved, her small hands expertly tying the bandages around the splint and my arm.

Rain seemed to be doing well, as did her pups. She rested a lot, her strength slowly returning. It was a miracle, witnessing life flourish in these dreary times.

Thunder, ever vigilant, took up the role of sentinel, keeping watch over our temporary sanctuary. We were safe, at least for now. Tonight, we sleep without fear, for tomorrow we march onwards, towards the unknown.

NOVEMBER 30, YEAR UNKNOWN

Today we made progress in an unexpected area - a mode of transportation for Rain's pups. Silence found an old rusty bicycle lying in a ditch nearby, its previous owner nowhere to be seen. Its use as a conventional bicycle was out of the question, given its dilapidated state. However, it had potential for something else.

Alongside the bike, we found an old wooden crate. After a bit of scavenging around, I managed to find some old rope and tools. I put my mechanical knowledge to good use, something I didn't think would be relevant in a world like this. We fashioned the crate to the bicycle frame, creating a makeshift cart for the pups.

The puppies, although initially scared, eventually took to their new ride. It was a sight to see - a tinge of happiness breaking through the gloom. Silence giggled for the first time in a long while, and even Rain, though worn out, wagged her tail at the sight.

It was a small victory, but in a world like ours, we cling to these moments. It felt like a bit of our humanity returned today, a reminder of what we were fighting to regain. Tomorrow, we venture forth once again. With the pups in tow, we feel reinvigorated, ready for the journey ahead.

NOVEMBER 31, YEAR UNKNOWN

Exhausted. Silence and I scrounge for more food for Rain. The pups are voracious little parasites, but they are thriving, and Rain's strength returns with each passing day. We find an old storage cellar nearby, half-flooded but still holding cans of food. Not suitable for us, but perfect for Rain.

The cries of the newborn pups fill the air, a sound of life so rare in these times. It stirs something within me, memories of another time when such sounds were commonplace. It's a reminder, too, of what's at stake, of what we're fighting to protect.

Thunder's hooves stamp impatiently outside. He's restless, sensing the encroaching danger even before I can hear it. Distant sounds, mechanical rumblings grow closer. We can't stay here for long. A sanctuary turned into a trap. The world reminding us we're not safe, not yet.

Evening sets in, and the sky bleeds a mournful shade of orange, stark against the lifeless grey around us. We've been lucky so far, but our luck might just be running out. Tomorrow, we move again.

DECEMBER 1, YEAR UNKNOWN

A long walk in the hot sun today. The scorched earth under our feet, the sky clear and unforgiving. Not a sign of any form of life around us, besides us four and the new additions.

I tried to communicate with Silence today. It's challenging, the gaps in understanding are wide, but we're closing them, slowly. She's a tough kid, brave and resilient. I saw her caring for the pups today. A maternal instinct shines through her, something that's still pure, untainted. It gives me hope.

Our journey is far from over. The danger still lingers, the unknown still awaits us. We need to keep moving, to keep surviving. As night falls, I look at them – Silence, Thunder, Rain, and the little ones. In this world of desolation, they have become my family. Our survival, our journey, it all means something now. The destination isn't clear, but the will to reach it is stronger than ever.

DECEMBER 2, YEAR UNKNOWN

More walking. More food for Rain. More silence. I watch her.
She's so small. So thin. But she never stops. Not for a moment.
She tends to Rain, to the pups. She's so strong. I feel... something.
Something I haven't felt in a long time. I think it's admiration.
Maybe even more. Is it possible? I don't know. All I know is that
I'll do anything to keep them safe. I have to keep them safe.
They're my... what? My family? I don't know. But they're mine.
And I'm theirs. I can't lose them. Not again.

DECEMBER 3, YEAR UNKNOWN

Rain is slowing us down. It's too soon for her to be walking so much. Silence and I take turns to carry her, but she prefers to walk. Slowly. With a mother's watchful eye on the pups.

DECEMBER 4, YEAR UNKNOWN

Today, we encountered a peculiar sight; a car, upside down, abandoned in the middle of nowhere. The sight of the car stirred within me the familiarity of the world that once was. But its pitiful state served as a stark reminder of our present reality. Even if I had two working arms to drive it, the once gleaming metal body was now rusted and beaten, its roof crushed under the weight of time and neglect. Its tires were long gone, and the fuel gauge pointed to almost empty. An ironic predicament for a car, I mused.

As I assessed the situation, Silence became noticeably restless. It was as if she had something to say but lacked the words. She pointed at herself, then the car, her young face taut with determination. It took me a moment, but then it dawned on me. She was older than she appeared, old enough to drive.

The spark of realization ignited a flame of hope. We could use the car! But the realization came with its own set of challenges. The car was upside down and needed to be righted. With my arm in a splint, it was a herculean task. But Thunder, unfazed by the obstacle, stood ready to assist. Together, we managed to flip the car over.

Once the car was upright, I went to inspect the engine, mentally preparing myself for the mechanical nightmare that awaited. But to my surprise, there was no engine. The space where it should have been was hollow, a gaping void.

A wave of disappointment washed over me, but it quickly receded, replaced by a new understanding. The absence of the engine was not a setback but an opportunity. The car was significantly lighter, light enough for Thunder to pull.

With the roof of the car removed, we had ample space. We put the pups on the backseat, their tiny bodies huddled together. Silence and Rain climbed into the front, their eyes reflecting the flicker of hope that lit up our hearts.

We didn't have an engine. We didn't have a pristine, smooth-riding vehicle. But we had a means to move forward, pulled by Thunder's relentless strength. The makeshift arrangement was far from perfect, but it was a step forward. A reminder that even amidst despair, ingenuity and hope could pave a path forward. Tomorrow, we continue our journey, a little closer to our destination, our spirits a little brighter.

DECEMBER 5, YEAR UNKNOWN

The day began like any other in this post-apocalyptic world. Thunder was hitched up, pulling our makeshift car, the pups snuggled in the back, Silence by my side. We were starting to get the hang of this peculiar setup. There was a rhythm to it now, a pattern that felt oddly comforting in the relentless uncertainty that clouded our days.

As we crunched along the desolate highway, the hot sun bore down on us. An oppressive silence hung in the air, broken only by the crunching of gravel under Thunder's hooves. The road ahead was long and winding, disappearing into the horizon.

And then, a speck in the distance caught my eye. At first, it seemed like an illusion, a mirage painted by the heat and my longing for human company. As we approached, the figure started to take shape. A man. Just sitting in the middle of the road. He looked weary, broken, his body slumped in defeat.

We halted our unusual procession. The sight of another living human being should have filled us with relief, perhaps even joy. But the world we now inhabited had taught us to be wary. Our survival depended on our ability to tread with caution. He was too far to have seen us.

As Silence clung to Rain a little tighter, we started to plan our next move. The man did not appear to be a threat, but appearances could be deceptive. He could be alone, or he could be a scout for a larger group, a trap to lure in unsuspecting wanderers like us.

We dared not approach. Not yet. There were too many variables, too many unknowns. The pups were our priority, their safety paramount. We decided to keep our distance, to watch and wait. Perhaps we could learn more about the man from afar. Perhaps the passing of time would reveal the truth of his intentions.

So, we spent the day in watchful anticipation, waiting for a sign, a clue that could tell us more about the man in the road. As the sun set, bathing the world in an eerie glow, we huddled together, alert and ready for whatever the coming night might bring.

DECEMBER 6, YEAR UNKNOWN

The night had been long and filled with the peculiar tension that accompanies the unknown. We had taken turns keeping watch, ensuring that the man on the road made no move towards us. He had stayed in the same position, motionless, until the early morning hours, when he fell onto his side, apparently succumbing to exhaustion.

As the morning light began to flood the desolate landscape, we stirred from our makeshift shelter. The pups were restless, picking up on our unease. Silence, in her usual compassionate way, had found a soft blanket among our scavenged items, and gently tucked them in. She remained with them, cooing softly, her soothing presence a buffer against the world outside.

We debated our next move. There were arguments to be made for both leaving and approaching. We could bypass the man entirely, veering off the road and continuing our journey. Yet, the image of him lying in the dirt pulled at something inside of me. A fragment of humanity that still lingered, still cared.

In the end, the decision was made. We would approach, but cautiously. We would give him a wide berth, ready to retreat at the first sign of danger. Thunder seemed to understand our intentions, as he always did, his intelligent eyes scanning the horizon for any threats.

As we slowly moved closer, I felt a peculiar mix of fear and hope. Fear for what we might encounter, hope for a potential ally in this desolate world. In the world we now inhabited, human contact was rare, precious. Yet, it also carried with it the potential for danger, for betrayal.

The man remained unmoving, oblivious to our approach. As we drew nearer, my heart pounded in my chest, every instinct screaming to be ready for a fight. But as we finally reached him, the sight that greeted us was not one of danger, but of pitiful desolation.

He was unconscious, his body ravaged by the harsh conditions. Whether he would wake up, whether we could even help him, remained to be seen. But for now, we had made our decision. We would not leave a fellow human to suffer alone in this unforgiving world. Not if we had a choice.

DECEMBER 7, YEAR UNKNOWN

Our morning began with a somber atmosphere, the presence of the unconscious man serving as a grim reminder of the world we lived in. He was dangerously thin, his skin stretched tight over his bones. His clothes were ragged, barely enough to protect him from the cold.

We quickly realised that we couldn't just leave him lying in the road. Not only was it dangerous for him, but also for us, since it made us a clear target for anyone or anything passing by. After a quick discussion, we decided to move him to the car. It was a challenge, given his size and my injured arm, but with Thunder's strength and Silence's determination, we managed it.

We placed him in the back seat with the pups, their innocent eyes watching with concern as we laid him out on the blankets. He remained unconscious, his chest rising and falling with shallow breaths. His condition was critical, and we could only do so much without proper medical supplies.

Silence busied herself with making him comfortable, adjusting his position and covering him with a blanket. I watched her, struck by her kindness and empathy. Despite everything she'd been through, she still cared, still tried to help. I admired her for that.

The rest of the day was spent foraging for food and water. We were running low, and with another mouth to feed, it became all the more crucial. Thunder and I went out, leaving Silence to watch over the man and the pups. It was a difficult task, our usual spots picked clean, but we managed to find enough for a few days.

As the day drew to a close, I found myself sitting by the man, watching his chest rise and fall. He was a stark reminder of the world we lived in, of the fragile line between life and death. We were all just one meal, one drink of water away from ending up like him. But we fought on, clinging to life, to each other, determined to survive.

Tomorrow, we would continue our journey, carrying the weight of our new responsibility. Whether the man survived was uncertain, but we would do our best. In this world, it was all we could do.

DECEMBER 8, YEAR UNKNOWN

As dawn broke, it was clear that our newest companion was in dire need of medical attention. Despite our best efforts to make him comfortable, his condition continued to worsen. His breaths were shallow and intermittent, his skin cold to the touch. There was an injury hidden beneath his clothes that we hadn't noticed before, an infection spreading with each passing hour.

A sense of urgency took over our small group. We needed to find a medical facility or at least some kind of medical supplies. But with the landscape barren and desolate, our options were limited. Silence and I exchanged worried glances as we packed our belongings, preparing to set out in search for aid.

We came across a dilapidated town after a few hours of travelling. Among the collapsed buildings and overgrown streets, we spotted a building that bore the faint symbol of a cross - a symbol of hope in our dire situation. Though it was difficult to tell from the outside, we hoped that it had once been a hospital or a clinic.

We left the man in the relative safety of the car with Rain and the pups. Safe enough under the watchful eye of our formidable four legged immovable object, while Silence and I ventured towards the building. It was eerily quiet as we navigated through the collapsed entrance, the faint scent of decay hanging in the air. But we pushed onwards, our need for medical supplies outweighing our fear.

We scavenged through the building, our search yielding a few precious medical supplies - antibiotics, bandages, antiseptic, even a few syringes. It wasn't much, but it was better than nothing. We quickly made our way back to the car, our hearts pounding in our chests.

The rest of the day was spent trying to administer aid to the man. We cleaned his wound, applied the antiseptic and bandaged it as best we could, hoping the antibiotics would help fight the infection. It was a grueling task, one that left us all exhausted by the time nightfall came. But we had done what we could.

As I sat by the man's side, watching him drift in and out of consciousness, I couldn't help but feel a sense of admiration for him. Despite his condition, despite the odds, he was fighting, clinging onto life with a tenacity that was inspiring. It was a reminder of the human spirit, of our determination to survive, to endure, no matter the circumstances.

Tomorrow, we continue on our journey, our resolve strengthened by the challenges we've overcome. And perhaps, with a little luck, our new companion will pull through.

DECEMBER 9, YEAR UNKNOWN

The storms returned today, bringing with them a torrential downpour that turned the landscape into a muddy, impassable wasteland. Our progress was significantly hindered, the car bogging down in the thick mud. Despite Thunder's strength, it was impossible to proceed with the car in this weather. We were forced to make the difficult decision to abandon it, a decision that brought us much distress considering our ailing companion.

We sought shelter from the storm in a nearby underground metro station, its entrance partially collapsed but accessible. With great effort, we managed to carry our unconscious companion down the treacherous steps, his labored breathing echoing off the damp, decaying walls. We settled in as comfortably as we could, using our limited supplies to create a makeshift bed for him. Rain and her pups huddled together for warmth, their whimpers barely audible over the roar of the storm above.

The underground station provided some semblance of protection, its abandoned, haunting halls offering us a refuge from the storm. Silence ventured to explore the further recesses of the station, her curious nature unable to resist the mystery of the darkened tunnels. Thunder, ever watchful, stood guard at the entrance, his imposing silhouette a reassurance in these uncertain times.

Our meal consisted of scavenged canned goods, our appetite dampened by the grim situation. We sat in silence, our thoughts occupied by the task at hand - keeping our companion alive and planning our next course of action once the storm subsided.

Tonight, as I write this entry, the sound of the storm seems distant, muffled by the concrete and steel that surrounds us. The man's breaths are shallow but steady, the fever seeming to have subsided slightly. There's hope yet, a glimmer amidst the gloom.

Tomorrow, we face whatever the new day brings. The storm will pass, as all storms do, and we'll emerge stronger, resilient. This journey has taught us much about the world, about ourselves, but most importantly, about the enduring strength of the human spirit. And as long as that spirit endures, we'll keep moving forward.

DECEMBER 10, YEAR UNKNOWN

The storm worsened today, escalating into a full-blown tornado that tore through the town above. We could hear the howl of the wind, the crashing and breaking of structures as they succumbed to the storm's fury. A mixture of dread and fascination held us captive as we listened to the tempest wreak havoc above ground.

Water started seeping into the metro station, an insidious, creeping flood that forced us further into the labyrinth of tunnels. The world above was crumbling, and yet, we had no other option but to delve deeper into the darkness below.

Carrying our companion was a task in itself. Despite his frailty, maneuvering him through the narrow passages was challenging. Silence and I took turns, one leading the way with a flashlight, the other ensuring our friend was as comfortable as possible. Rain was clearly agitated, her instincts sensing the danger. She stayed close, her pups bundled tightly in Silence's arms. Thunder followed us, his massive form barely fitting in some of the smaller tunnels.

As we journeyed deeper, the eerie quiet of the underground was unsettling. The only sounds were our own breaths, the dripping water, and the faint, distant echoes of the storm above. We found an old maintenance room, its door barely hanging on its hinges. It was dry and relatively clean, a suitable place to set up camp.

We made do with what we had, our supplies dwindling with each passing day. The man was barely conscious now, his eyes fluttering open only occasionally. We did what we could, cleaning his wound and changing his bandages. His life was in our hands, and we were determined to see him through.

Despite the circumstances, there was a sense of unity, of shared determination. We were survivors in a world that had turned against us, yet we were fighting. We were surviving. The storm above could rage on, but it wouldn't break us. In the darkness of the metro station, we found not just shelter, but resolve. The storm will pass, and when it does, we'll continue our journey, battered but unbroken.

DECEMBER 11, YEAR UNKNOWN

The storm raged on today, its fury unabated. The wind roared above us like a wrathful beast, its voice echoing through the underground. It was a constant reminder of the world we left above, a world being reshaped by Mother Nature's anger.

In the midst of it all, we found an unexpected distraction. Buried beneath a pile of discarded items in the corner of the room was an old radio. A relic from a time when communication was a matter of convenience, not survival. It was a dusty, worn-out piece, its dials and knobs all but faded. But to us, it was a beacon of hope, a possible lifeline to the outside world.

We gathered around the radio, its presence a break from the grim reality. I fiddled with the knobs, my hands shaking with anticipation and uncertainty. After a series of static and white noise, a voice pierced through. A man, filled with passion and fervor, preaching about the undead, calling them the banished, the unholy.

His words were a mix of fear, faith, and madness. He painted a picture of a world judged and found wanting, its people paying the ultimate price. It was surreal, a voice from the void, a voice of desperation and unwavering belief.

Silence and I looked at each other, the reality of the situation sinking in. We were not alone in this apocalypse. There were others, holding onto their beliefs, their hope, their sanity. It was a reminder of our shared humanity, our shared struggles.

Rain, sensing our heightened emotions, came over, her pups trotting behind her. She nudged my hand, a silent gesture of solidarity. Our companion, although weak, managed a faint smile. We were in this together, bound by our shared hope and determination.

The storm continued to rage outside, but in the dim light of the maintenance room, we found comfort. In the fervent voice of the radio preacher, we found connection. Tomorrow, we journey again, reminded of the world that was, the world that is, and the world that could be. No matter what lies ahead, we'll face it together.

DECEMBER 12, YEAR UNKNOWN

The man woke up today, his eyes wild with fear and confusion. He scrambled back against the wall when he saw me, screams echoing through the tunnels. "Beast! Beast!" he cried out, his voice filled with panic and terror. I felt a pang in my chest, a sharp reminder of the monster I had become.

But then, something unexpected happened. Silence stepped between the man and me, her movements gentle and careful. She took his trembling hand and placed it on her belly. She then mouthed something, two syllables that I didn't quite catch. The man repeated the word, his voice trembling, "Baby."

At that moment, everything fell into place. I felt as if the world had come to a sudden halt. The 'baby'. I had thought all along that the baby was somewhere else, lost, and Silence had been desperately trying to find it. The truth was far different, far more profound. The baby wasn't out there. It was growing inside her.

Suddenly, my quest to find a baby, our journey, took on a completely new meaning. All the while, I had been looking for someone who didn't exist yet. It wasn't about finding. It was about protecting, about ensuring a future. I looked at Silence, her eyes glistening in the faint light. She was carrying hope itself within her.

The man's panic seemed to have subsided. The connection with a new life, an innocent life, seemed to have calmed him. He stared at me quietly, but I was too stunned to respond. I simply nodded.

We're not just surviving now. We're safeguarding a future. The burden feels heavier, the mission even more critical. Tomorrow, we press on with renewed purpose, and I am filled with a strange blend of fear and hope.

DECEMBER 13, YEAR UNKNOWN

The storms have ceased for now, leaving behind a world battered and torn. We emerged from the tunnels, blinking in the harsh, unforgiving light of a new day. The little town we'd left behind had been transformed into a wasteland by the tornado. Buildings were crushed, cars tossed like toys, and streets flooded with murky water.

Silence, the man, and I stared at the scene in front of us, each of us lost in our thoughts. There was a surreal quality to the destruction, a stark reminder of the volatile world we were living in. It wasn't just the zombies; nature itself seemed determined to eradicate any traces of the past.

The pups whined, uneasy amidst the ruins. Rain, although still recovering, seemed determined to push forward, leading the pack with a surprising show of strength. We had to leave the car behind, buried under layers of debris and mud. It was a loss, but not one that could not be overcome. Thunder, resilient as ever, seemed ready to resume his duties.

Despite the havoc, there was an eerie beauty in the devastation. The once familiar was now alien, each object a relic from a time that now seemed distant. We were strangers in a strange land, journeying through the remnants of a world that had once been ours.

We scoured for any useful supplies amongst the wreckage, but there was little to be found. The medical building we had hoped to find was now a shell, its walls collapsed and interior laid bare. The man's injury would have to wait.

As night approached, we decided to move on, leaving the broken town behind. Tomorrow holds a new set of challenges, and we need to be ready.

DECEMBER 14, YEAR UNKNOWN

Today was surprisingly peaceful, considering our current circumstances. The man, who introduced himself as Whisky, chattered away cheerfully to Silence as we journeyed on. He perched comfortably on Thunder, the two seemingly forming a bond of their own. Whisky's energy was infectious, his stories from the 'old world' bringing a bit of color to our dreary existence.

Silence listened to Whisky with interest, her eyes twinkling. It was comforting to see her engage with someone who could speak. I felt content just watching them, a quiet observer to their interactions. The pups played at our feet, Rain kept a watchful eye on them, while I watched over all. Our little family was growing, and it felt good.

Whisky revealed that his name was a nickname from a past life. A time when alcohol-induced problems were the biggest worries, not surviving each day. His confession prompted me to think about my own name - Lance.

Suddenly, I was hit by a crippling headache, like a hot knife slicing through my brain. It was excruciating, taking me down to my knees. Flashes of memories passed before my eyes, as if a dam had broken. Not my name, but my rank, my role – Lance Corporal. I was a soldier, a second in command. A guardian, a protector...

As my past collided with my present, my vision blurred. The last thing I remember was the sunlight growing too bright to bear, a piercing white against the dull greys of our world. Then everything went dark.

I woke up later, the headache reduced to a dull throb. Whisky and Silence hovered over me, concern etched on their faces. I smiled weakly, indicating that I was alright. Today had been a revelation, a key to a part of me that was lost. I was Lance, and this was my fight.

As the sun set, we found a relatively safe spot to camp for the night. As I fight off sleep, I find myself strangely excited for the new day, for the unknown trials and revelations it may bring. My past is returning, and I am ready to face it.

DECEMBER 15, YEAR UNKNOWN

Today was another day of pressing on, of moving forward against the odds. It was just an average day, until the afternoon when the shrill sound of engines filled the air. We looked up in unison, as a group of aircrafts soared across the sky. They were flying low, disturbingly low. It was the first time we'd seen anything like that since the outbreak.

We froze on the spot, not sure what to do. We were in plain sight, the late afternoon sun casting long shadows of our huddled group on the open road. There was nowhere to hide, no time to run. Our hearts pounded as we watched the planes fly overhead, disappearing into the horizon as quickly as they had appeared.

Silence, fear evident in her eyes, clutched at her belly protectively. Whisky looked equally concerned, while Thunder and Rain were visibly agitated. The pups, unaware of the danger, continued their play, their innocence a sharp contrast to our grim reality.

Had they seen us? Were we now a target? A myriad of questions raced through our minds, each more alarming than the previous. But there was nothing we could do but press on, and hope for the best. So, that's what we did. We gathered our belongings, tightened our grips on our makeshift weapons, and continued our journey.

The rest of the day was filled with an underlying tension that had us on edge. Every noise, every rustle seemed amplified, setting off alarm bells in our minds. As night fell, we chose a hidden spot for camp, taking extra precautions.

The feeling of being potentially watched, hunted even, was a new level of fear. But we had no choice but to confront it, to adapt and keep going. As I write this, I can't help but look up at the sky, wondering what the morning will bring. One thing is certain, the journey is far from over.

DECEMBER 16, YEAR UNKNOWN

Tonight, we witnessed the stark return of an old threat, reminding us once again of the relentless and watchful presence of an enemy we can't seem to shake off.

As the last glow of the setting sun vanished behind the mountains, replaced by the inky blanket of night, we noticed pinpricks of light dancing across the desert ground. Upon looking up, we saw them - drones. Silent as specters and equally menacing, they hovered in the night sky, their spotlights tracing ghostly fingers over the barren landscape. Searching for us after the fly-by? Were we seen?

Each passing minute was filled with the chilling dread of exposure. We stayed as still as the rocks around us, praying the drones wouldn't detect our presence. Rain and her pups were silent, hidden in the shadow of a nearby rock formation. Whisky, Thunder and Silence huddled together, barely daring to breathe. I sat guard over Rain as she slept, her pups moaning softly in their sleep.

The drones continued their relentless search, sweeping back and forth, their mechanical humming disturbing the natural symphony of the night. But as hours slipped away, they moved further from our location. Hope slowly crept back, whispering promises of another day survived, another danger averted.

When dawn broke, painting the sky with shades of pink and gold, the drones were gone. As much as the sunrise brought a sense of relief, it also served as a harsh reminder of the reality we were living in. The light of day brought no promise of safety, only the guarantee of another day to survive, another set of challenges to face.

The drones might have gone for now, but their ominous presence hangs over us like a shroud, casting long shadows even in the bright light of day. We must stay vigilant, for we never know when they might return.

DECEMBER 17, YEAR UNKNOWN

I woke with a start in the early hours. A strange sound had pierced the silence of the desert night - a distant humming, growing gradually louder. I peered into the inky darkness. Then, the ground lit up with sweeping spotlights. Drones.

They were back.

With a jolt of adrenaline, I urged everyone to keep as quiet as possible and bury themselves under the sand. We could only hope that our heat signatures would be masked by the cold desert sand. The drone's ominous hum was omnipresent, casting a shadow of terror that even the darkness of the night couldn't compete with.

Whisky was trembling, not so much from the cold, but from pure, unfiltered fear. I could see it mirrored in Silence's eyes as well, although she was trying to remain composed for the sake of Whisky and the pups. Rain, ever the protective mother, shielded her young ones under her body.

As the drones moved closer, sweeping their spotlights in our direction, I could feel my heart pounding in my chest. This was it. This was how we would be found out. A fear, unlike anything I'd experienced before, washed over me.

Suddenly, as quickly as they had come, the drones began to recede. Their sinister hum dwindling into the distance, the terror of their spotlights replaced once again by the comforting cloak of desert darkness.

In the silence that followed, I could hear everyone's sighs of relief. It felt as though we'd been holding our breaths collectively. The drones were gone. We were safe, for now.

But as I laid my head back onto the sand, I couldn't shake off the feeling of dread. The drones were a reminder of the eyes that were constantly on the lookout for survivors, or worse, any signs of the infected. We were a walking target, and the journey to the facility seemed even more daunting now.

DECEMBER 18, YEAR UNKNOWN

The cold desert morning hit us hard today. Without the shelter of our makeshift vehicle, we're exposed to the elements. Silence is stoic as ever, wrapping herself tighter in the ragged blankets we managed to salvage. Thunder seems unfazed by the temperature, but Whisky isn't faring well, and Rain sticks close for warmth.

In our path, we discovered an abandoned shopping trolley, rusted and weather-beaten. After a quick inspection and some minor repairs, we found it sturdy enough to transport Rain's pups. Rain, protective as ever, inspected the trolley cautiously before finally allowing her little ones to nestle in. It was a moment of slight relief amidst the harsh reality of our journey.

As we walked, we crossed paths with the skeleton of a forgotten desert town, its eerie silence broken only by the howling wind. It's a grim reminder of the world we've lost. There's no time to linger, though. The sight of drones yesterday has put us all on edge. We need to keep moving. We have to reach that research facility, our beacon of hope, as quickly as possible.

But we have another priority now. Silence's belly is growing by the day. We must find a safe place before her time comes. Despite the unknowns that lie ahead, we trudge forward - a strange little family bound by circumstances, walking together through the ruins of the world.

DECEMBER 19, YEAR UNKNOWN

We walked through most of the morning and afternoon, resting occasionally to let Whisky and the pups regain strength. The sun was relentless, beating down upon us with an intensity I hadn't experienced before. The heat was stifling, but we had to push on.

Silence took turns with Whisky in guiding the trolley. Every now and then, she would stop to check on the pups, ensuring they were comfortable and shaded from the harsh sun. It's fascinating to see her with them - this quiet, resilient girl who hadn't uttered a word since I met her, showing such tender care for these tiny beings.

As the day wore on, Whisky, his health waning, struggled to keep pace. I offered to pull the trolley, but he insisted on helping. "I'm still good for something," he muttered, his face lined with determination. He wasn't the only one with health concerns, though. I have noticed Silence's gait slowing down, her hand often resting on her belly. We'll need to find a safe place for her soon.

Tonight, we set up camp at the outskirts of an old abandoned farm. As I write this, Whisky is telling stories to Silence by the firelight, her eyes wide with wonder. It's a heartwarming sight, one that takes me back to simpler times. Times when life was about living, not just surviving.

Tomorrow, we march again, our hearts heavy but hopeful. To whatever the future holds, we face it together.

DECEMBER 20, YEAR UNKNOWN

The farm offered us a welcome respite, the abandoned barn giving us shelter from the bitter cold that has taken hold with the onset of winter. It's strange to think about seasons, about how the earth still turns and the sun still rises and sets, even as the world we knew crumbles.

In the morning, we made an important discovery: a small reservoir of water at the back of the farm. We filled our bottles and canteens, gave Thunder a hearty drink and also managed to bathe the pups, something that I think they appreciated more than we did.

Whisky, who seems to grow weaker with each passing day, surprised us by catching a rabbit. We cooked it over an open fire, and for the first time in a long time, we had a proper meal. Whisky joked about the old times, about steaks and Sunday roasts, and for a moment, it almost felt like we were just a group of friends out on a camping trip, not survivors in a post-apocalyptic world.

Silence, ever the caretaker, took care of the pups.

As the day ended, and as we huddled together in the barn, I realized something. This strange group of misfits, we've become a family of sorts. And it gives me hope. Hope that despite everything, life can go on. Life will go on. Tomorrow, we journey onward.

DECEMBER 21, YEAR UNKNOWN

Today, something rather strange happened. As we were preparing to leave the farm, we found a peculiar object half buried in the earth: a satellite phone. It looked incredibly out of place in the rural setting of the farm, like a relic of a bygone era.

Initially, I thought it was useless, another electronic device rendered obsolete by the apocalypse. But then I noticed the small solar panel on the back. After clearing off the dust and grime, we left it out in the sun. It took a few hours, but eventually, the screen flickered to life.

Whisky, who had been a tech enthusiast in his past life, couldn't contain his excitement. With deft fingers, he navigated the archaic menus and got to a screen that indicated the phone's signal strength. It was weak, but it was there.

We spent the afternoon taking turns hollering into the phone, shouting our 'hello's. It felt silly and desperate, yet liberating. For the first time since the world fell apart, we felt connected, even if just theoretically, to other survivors out there.

We didn't receive any response today. But now that we have a means of communication, we feel an odd mix of anticipation and anxiety. Who might respond? Would they be friend or foe? We've decided to try again tomorrow. Until then, the phone will be charging under the winter sun.

Despite the lack of a concrete response, today has felt like a victory. As if we're not just surviving, but taking steps towards reclaiming the world. Tonight, we rest with a new sense of hope, and tomorrow, we continue our journey.

DECEMBER 22, YEAR UNKNOWN

Today, with Whisky feeling unwell, we decided to remain at the farm, using the time for recovery and rest. Thunder and Rain, who had been somewhat restless in the unfamiliar surroundings, finally seemed to settle down. The pups played with each other in the yard, their carefree joy a stark contrast to the harsh world they had been born into.

It was during this downtime that Whisky shared his tale. I had always wondered what he had been doing when the world ended, and today he revealed the harrowing story. He was at his computer, in the shadow of Silicon Valley, working on a software update for a small tech startup when the first news reports came in. The details were sketchy, but it was enough to send panic rippling through the office.

In the following weeks, as society collapsed and chaos ensued, Whisky survived by making smart decisions and learning quickly. He learned to scavenge for food and supplies, to avoid large cities, and to stay on the move. When things got worse, he somehow managed to keep his humanity intact, helping others when he could, seldom stealing or causing harm.

As Whisky recounted his journey, Silence sat by his side, her hand on her stomach. She didn't understand the words, but she understood the emotion behind them. They were stories of survival, resilience, and the human spirit.

Today reminded me that we are more than just survivors. We are the last carriers of human history, each of us with our own stories to tell. Tonight, we rest under the winter sky, our thoughts lingering on the world that was, and the world that might yet be.

DECEMBER 23, YEAR UNKNOWN

Not today.

DECEMBER 24, YEAR UNKNOWN

The entry I make today is one I hoped I wouldn't have to. Yesterday morning, with the first light of day, Whisky passed away.

Despite our best efforts, the infection was too much for his body to handle. His fever never broke. Throughout the night, he would occasionally stir, murmuring things under his breath. His sleep was restless, troubled. And then, when the first light of dawn peeked in, he simply stopped breathing.

I can't shake off the silence that his departure has left. Whisky's incessant chatter, his words of wisdom and sprinklings of humor, had become a comforting part of our lives in a short time. Now, his absence is a raw, gaping hole in our group.

Silence, true to her name, has not said anything. She simply sat by Whisky, holding his hand until it turned cold. The look on her face, however, spoke volumes - grief, pain, and a deep sense of loss. It was a reflection of how I felt inside.

We buried Whisky today, marking his grave with an old Whisky bottle we found in our travels - a tribute he would have appreciated. As we said our goodbyes, I couldn't help but feel the sting of his loss. Whisky was a survivor, a fighter till the end. But this world... it seems, it spares no one.

Tonight, we sleep under a cloud of grief, the loss of Whisky weighing heavily on our hearts. Yet, we persist, for that is what he would have wanted. We carry forward his memory, his strength, and his determination. The journey continues, albeit with a heavy heart.

DECEMBER 25, YEAR UNKNOWN

Today, we walked in silence. Each footstep we took echoed the rhythm of our heavy hearts. Every mile traversed felt like a tribute to Whisky, a way of carrying forward his memory.

The landscape around us seemed to mimic our somber mood. The ruins of the old world, the barrenness, it all felt symbolic of the loss we had suffered. There were no conversations today, no chatter to fill the silence. Instead, we let our grief walk with us, a silent companion in our journey.

Even the pups, usually a source of much-needed cheer, seemed to sense the mood. They stayed quiet in their makeshift trolley, their small eyes watching us with what seemed like understanding. Rain, too, was quieter than usual, sticking close to Silence as we made our way forward.

By nightfall, we made camp under the shelter of an old, dilapidated building. The air was chilly, the wind carrying whispers of the winter to come. As we huddled together for warmth, the silence seemed louder, the emptiness more palpable.

Today, we mourned. We allowed ourselves to feel the pain, the loss. But tomorrow, we must move forward. For Whisky, for ourselves, for the hope of a better world that we're journeying towards.

Tonight, as I close this entry, I can't help but think of Whisky's unyielding spirit, his undying hope in the face of adversity. His memory strengthens our resolve. It reminds us why we're on this journey.

We rest tonight. Tomorrow, we walk again.

DECEMBER 26, YEAR UNKNOWN

Today was a struggle. Not the usual kind of struggle we've grown accustomed to, but a struggle against a steadfast will. That of Thunder's.

For the first time since we found him, Thunder refused to move. We tried to coax him, Silence and I, with tender words and gentle pats. Even Rain joined in, her nose nudging his, as if to encourage him. But it was all to no avail. The usually obedient creature, the symbol of strength in our small group, stood firmly, his hooves planted on the frost-covered ground.

His refusal to move was not out of exhaustion or sickness. No, his eyes were clear, his body still strong. It was as if he was mourning in his own way, paying respect to the man who'd ridden him, who'd passed away so suddenly. His stubbornness was a symbol of his grief, of his respect for Whisky.

It was a somber realization for all of us. In our grief, we'd overlooked that our four-legged companions too were feeling the loss. That they too mourned the absence of the jovial man who'd quickly become a part of our strange family.

We decided to camp there for the day, letting Thunder have his moment of silence, his day of mourning. There was a small clearing nearby, shielded from the wind by a copse of bare trees. We gathered what we could to build a fire and huddled close, our bodies seeking comfort in the shared warmth.

Tonight, as I write this entry by the dying fire, I look over to Thunder. The large creature is silhouetted against the moonlit night, his gaze far-off. Tomorrow, we'll try to move again. For now, we let him mourn in peace. After all, loss and grief are universal - be it human or horse.

DECEMBER 27, YEAR UNKNOWN

Today, we woke to a harsh reality. The already grating cold seemed to bite a bit more viciously, and the world was a shade bleaker. Thunder was gone.

His absence was glaring, a hollow space where a large, warm presence used to be. He had left sometime during the night, without a sound, without a trace. I spent the better part of the morning looking for him, calling out his name into the stark, white wilderness. But there was no response. Only the biting wind answered back, carrying away my words.

Silence was as distraught as I was, maybe more. She'd grown close to the horse, often found whispering to him, sharing her thoughts, her fears. To her, Thunder was not just a beast of burden, but a friend, a confidant.

Rain seemed anxious too, the pups whining and huddling closer to her. They'd grown accustomed to the horse's large protective shadow. Now, they looked about nervously, as if expecting danger to spring from the vacant space Thunder used to occupy.

There was no choice but to move on. The weather had taken a turn for the worse. Fat, lazy snowflakes started falling sometime around noon, growing in intensity as the day wore on. The world was slowly getting draped in a thick layer of white, our path becoming more and more difficult to tread.

We packed up the trolley with what we could carry, Rain's pups snugly nestled among the rags and remnants of our past journey. Silence took the lead, pulling the trolley with a determination that I couldn't help but admire. I followed, Rain at my heel, our journey taking on a new, grim determination.

Thunder, if you're out there, stay safe, friend. We press on, bearing the weight of your absence, but the memory of your companionship lightens the burden.

DECEMBER 28, YEAR UNKNOWN

Our morning began in terror. A screeching convoy of army trucks, loaded with gun-toting survivors, came tearing down the road. The sudden, brutal noise ripped through the morning's calm, and within moments, we were surrounded.

The survivors weren't interested in conversation. They overpowered me with sheer numbers, their laughter echoing off the skeletal remains of buildings. Silence watched in horror from the sidelines, clutching the pups close to her chest. Fear painted a stark picture on her face. She was helpless. We all were.

The torment seemed to stretch on endlessly, each moment a drawn-out nightmare. And then, the unexpected happened. A familiar neigh tore through the cacophony. Thunder, in all his magnificent fury, barrelled through the crowd of marauders. And upon his back was a sight straight out of a horror tale, but in that moment, it was the most welcome sight in the world - Whisky, the man we had mourned, now an undead avenger.

Whisky, with a savage roar, swung his arm at the closest form and so beheaded the leader of their pack. Panic erupted among the others. They fled in all directions, then attempted to retaliate, while a couple stood frozen in shock. Thunder, with Whisky still on his back, led the men away, a terrifying, grim specter of retribution.

With the marauders distracted, we wasted no time. We gathered our belongings and darted into the nearby woods, the dense foliage providing a much-needed cover. The chilling laughter and screams of the survivors faded into the distance, replaced by the soothing hum of nature.

It was a narrow escape, one that cost us the illusion of safety. But tonight, as we huddle together in the heart of the forest, the crackling fire casting flickering shadows over our anxious faces, we're just grateful to be alive. To be together. And we owe it all to

Thunder and Whisky, our unlikely saviors.

DECEMBER 29, YEAR UNKNOWN

Our hearts weigh heavy today as we tread carefully through the winter-stripped trees. Yesterday's encounter with the marauders shook us, leaving a cold pit of fear in our stomachs. Despite our miraculous escape, we are reminded of the constant dangers lurking around every corner.

While we had hoped to see Thunder again, the possibility of Whisky's return poses a major concern. If he is a true undead, as his appearance suggested, we cannot risk having him in our midst, not with Silence and the pups. The very thought sends a shiver down my spine.

So today, as we moved slowly but steadily across the snowy landscape, we kept a constant lookout. Every rustle of the wind, every crunch of our footsteps in the snow seemed amplified, our senses on high alert. But there was no sign of Thunder or Whisky.

The day passed in relative silence, save for our soft footfalls and the occasional whimpering of the pups. We miss Thunder's steady presence. But for now, it's a relief not to see them. It's a bitter truth we swallow as we set up camp for the night under the pale, watchful eyes of the moon. We're safe, for now, and that's all we can ask for in these troubling times.

DECEMBER 30, YEAR UNKNOWN

The snow intensified today, a chilling white blanket smothering the earth. Each step we took felt heavy, our journey a slow trudge through the winter landscape. Visibility is limited, but the stark, silent beauty of the snow-covered world couldn't be missed. The pups seemed intrigued by the change in scenery, their curious sniffs and attempts to touch the cold white crystals a momentary distraction from our grim reality.

Midday, a drone whirred overhead, the familiar, cold mechanical hum breaking through the peaceful silence. It was an unsettling reminder that we were potentially being watched, hunted even. But its sudden appearance also presented an opportunity. Whoever controlled these drones must have resources, perhaps even a shelter. It might even lead us to the facility we've been searching for.

The drone continued its path, oblivious to our presence. We took a collective breath and made the decision to follow it. It was a risk, we knew, but every step we took in this world was a gamble. As the drone became a speck in the snowy expanse, we hurriedly packed our things and set off in its direction, the pups nestled securely in their trolley, Rain trudging alongside us, her breath misting in the freezing air.

By nightfall, we had made some progress, but the drone was long out of sight. Our hopes rested on the fact that drones usually operate within a limited range, so we must be getting closer to... something, or someone. As we huddled together for warmth, the bitter cold seeping into our bones, we couldn't help but let a sliver of hope warm our hearts. Perhaps tomorrow would bring us closer to a place of safety, to answers, to a future. Only time would tell.

DECEMBER 31, YEAR UNKNOWN

With the biting cold growing harsher, and the snow turning deeper, we had to rethink our means of travel today. Silence, visibly weary, struggled to keep pace with us, her petite frame burdened by her growing belly. The puppies, too, found the snow a challenge, their small bodies barely keeping above the drifts.

As we trudged on, we came across the remains of an old sled, half buried in the snow. The sight sparked an idea. We spent the better part of the morning rigging the sled, using the ropes we had and strengthening the structure with bits of wood and metal we found scattered nearby.

Once ready, we carefully placed the pups on the sled, tucking them in snugly with the rags we'd scavenged. Silence hesitated, but one look at her drained face made it clear she needed the rest. She climbed on, nestling among the puppies, her hand protectively on her belly.

Rain and I shared the duty of pulling the sled, the task made somewhat easier by the slick snow underfoot. We trekked in silence, each lost in our thoughts, our breath fogging in the frigid air. Even in the heart of this frozen wasteland, we found warmth in the image of our makeshift family, safely tucked in the sled behind us.

Nightfall found us huddled together, the shared body warmth warding off the icy cold. As we drifted into an uneasy sleep, I couldn't help but feel a sense of satisfaction. Despite the challenges, we were moving forward, together, one day at a time. Tomorrow, we'll press on. The facility, and hopefully a better future, awaits.

JANUARY 3, YEAR UNKNOWN

Today was a day of quiet contemplation. As we tread through the snow, my mind kept circling back to the beginning of this journey. I remember waking up, alone and frightened, in an unfamiliar world. I remember the overwhelming desperation, the yearning to find someone, anyone, who was like me - undead, yet conscious. I believed that if I could just find another like me, I could piece together the puzzle of my existence.

But now, things are different. I no longer search for answers about myself; instead, my focus has shifted entirely towards the family I've found. Silence, with her unborn child. Rain, and her adorable pups. They've become my world, my anchor in this sea of chaos.

I can still feel the decay in my veins, the pull of the undead's curse. And as I watch over Silence, her belly swelling with new life, I find myself hoping with a fervor I didn't know I was capable of. I hope to find a cure - not for myself, but for them. For this family that I never expected, but now cannot imagine being without.

I realize now that my journey has transformed from a quest for personal answers to a desperate race against time. For every day that passes, the baby grows closer to birth, and the stakes rise. I'm no longer just an undead man seeking answers, I'm a protector, a guardian.

As night falls, I sit beside the dwindling fire, lost in thought. The smell of the undead still lingers in the air, a grim reminder of what's at stake. But it only strengthens my resolve. I will find a cure. I must. For them. For us.

JANUARY 6, YEAR UNKNOWN

A shroud of unease has settled over me. My mind is troubled, constantly churning with fragments of a thought that I just can't seem to grasp. It's like an itch I can't reach, persistent and irritating. My nights are filled with dreams, more vivid and intense than usual.

In my dream, I see myself walking on the frozen lake once again. The ice beneath me is thin and brittle. Suddenly, it cracks and I fall through. Icy water engulfs me, and for a moment, all I see is a blue expanse. Then I feel a hand, grabbing me, pulling me out. But when I break through the surface, there's no one there.

I awake, breathless and soaked in sweat. Silence is there, as always, watching me with worried eyes. I offer her a reassuring smile, but my unease lingers. My arm throbs with pain, reminding me of the fall and the damage that was done. I feel a tinge of fear at the memory, fear of that sudden loss of control, the sinking feeling of being pulled under.

The day ahead is daunting. The sight of the frozen undead in the valley is still fresh in our minds, and the thought of what lies ahead brings with it a cold dread. But we press on. We have to.

As we walk, I can't shake off the feeling that I'm forgetting something important, something crucial. I run through our plans, our supplies, our route, but nothing stands out. It gnaws at me, but I push it to the back of my mind. There's no time for uncertainty now. We have a long way to go and a mission to complete.

Tonight, as I prepare for another restless sleep, I wonder if the dream will return. I hope that it holds the answer to the nagging thought that I've been missing. But for now, all I can do is close my eyes and wait for what the night brings. The day was warmer at least.

JANUARY 7, YEAR UNKNOWN

There's a chill in the air today, not just from the cold but from something far more sinister. The moans of the undead echoed in the darkness, a haunting chorus that sent shivers down our spines. Their numbers seemed to increase with every passing minute, the volume of their collective cries growing ever more daunting.

What terrified me more was the ground beneath us. The cold, hard snow was now damp under my hands, a sign of the impending doom we were about to face. The realization hit me like a gut punch - the valley of the dead was melting. The icy tomb that held the undead was losing its grip, and soon, it would release its horrifying prisoners.

We have to move, and we have to move fast. Panic claws at my chest but I fight to keep it at bay. We need a plan. The safest place, the only place, is on the other side of the frozen lake. But to get there, we have to traverse through the valley once more before it fully thaws.

The prospect is terrifying. One misstep, one moment of distraction could be the end of us. The valley is a maze of frozen bodies, a twisted graveyard that's about to awaken. But there's no other option. We have to face the horror that lies ahead.

We spent the rest of the night making plans, outlining every possible scenario, every contingency we can think of. The air is heavy with tension, but there's a grim determination in all of us. We have come so far, faced so many challenges, and we will not let this stop us.

No sleep tonight, we are heading back toward the valley. The air is colder now, the night a little quieter and the journey ahead more daunting than ever. But we will press on. For each other, for our future, for the hope that keeps us going.

JANUARY 8, YEAR UNKNOWN

As dawn broke, we were greeted by an unexpected sight. Standing tall and mighty in our path was Thunder. His eyes, once full of warmth, were now hardened by the experiences he had been through. There was no sign of Whisky, which led me to believe that they must have parted ways.

Thunder regarded us carefully, his gaze lingering on the pups and Silence. After what seemed like an eternity, he nuzzled against Silence, a silent acceptance of his return to our group. We welcomed him back tentatively, unsure of what the future holds for us all.

With Thunder back by our side, we arrived at the edge of the valley. The sight was horrifying - a sea of snow that was slowly melting away, revealing the grisly sight of bodies frozen in their final moments of terror.

The air reeked of decay and death. The valley looked different, more sinister under the daylight. The figures in the snow were no longer obscured by the darkness of the night. They were laid bare for all to see, a grotesque display of what had once been humanity.

Despite the dread curling in my stomach, we steeled ourselves for the journey ahead. Thunder seemed to understand the severity of our situation. He was restless, his eyes constantly darting towards the valley.

As we ventured into the valley, the moans of the undead echoed around us, a grim reminder of what lies beneath our feet. But we pressed on, determined to reach the other side of the frozen lake. Our journey had just begun.

At the edge of the valley, we slowed right down, intending to navigate the treacherous path as silently as possible. The sled, laden with our supplies and the pups, was light enough for

Thunder to pull, his hooves treading softly on the icy terrain. The moans of the undead filled the air, echoing in a disconcerting symphony of dread. I could see the fear in Silence's eyes, a fear that mirrored my own. But we pressed on, moving as quietly and as quickly as we could.

One horrifying moment, Silence tumbled off her seat, her foot slipping into a hidden crevice in the snow. Instantly, a decaying hand shot out, grabbing hold of her ankle. She screamed, a sound of pure fright that cut through the chorus of undead moans like a knife.

The undead were awakening, their slumber disturbed by our intrusion. One by one, they began to rise, their groans growing louder and their movements more desperate. The valley was becoming alive with the dead.

In the chaos, I had a flash of inspiration. I tied the sled securely to Thunder, and Thunder seemed to understand, a fire set in his eyes. Silence and Rain hopped onto the Sled and I threw myself into the mob, drawing the undead away from Thunder and the makeshift cart. Thunder took off, pulling the sled and its precious cargo away from danger.

In the midst of the undead, I found myself alone again. But this time, it was by choice. I watched as Thunder disappeared into the distance, taking Silence and the dogs with him. I felt a pang of loss, but also a sense of relief. They were safe, at least for now. And that was all that mattered. I could deal with being alone. I've done it before. I can do it again.

Now, as I sit in a lousy excuse for a shelter away from the valley, I can only hope that they make it to the other side of the lake, away from this waking nightmare. I finally managed to tear the grasping hands away from me. Crunching, screaming. I hope I bought them some time. They are everything to me. They are my family. There was no sight of them. Today was hell, but we survived it, and that's what matters. Tomorrow, I will find them.

For now, it's me, Lance, against the world. But I'm not giving up. Not yet.

JANUARY 9, YEAR UNKNOWN

A new year begins with a new challenge. The snow was falling heavily, making it difficult to follow Thunder's tracks. But I am no stranger to tracking - it's been a significant part of my survival so far.

I used my knowledge to look for signs of their passage. Broken branches, disturbed snow, anything that would indicate they had been there. Every so often, I'd find a print from Thunder's hooves, a tiny scrap of cloth from the sled, a shallow groove in the snow where the sled had been dragged - all subtle signs they had gone this way.

As the day progressed, I saw signs that they had to evade several undead - tracks that abruptly changed direction, signs of a scuffle. The frequency of these encounters worried me. The thawing of the valley was awakening more of the undead than I initially thought.

Yet, amidst the fear and the worry, there was also a sense of pride. They were evading, surviving. Silence was learning, adapting. I smiled at the thought of her, Rain, the pups and Thunder as a little team, surviving this harsh world. I could see her strength growing every day, could see her becoming a leader.

As the day ended, I had to stop, set up camp. I haven't found them yet, but I'm close, I can feel it. My heart aches with longing, but it is also filled with hope. I know they're out there, waiting for me. Tomorrow, I will find them. I promise.

JANUARY 10, YEAR UNKNOWN

This morning I awoke to a world painted white, a fresh blanket of snow hiding everything underneath. The beautiful, untouched landscape was deceiving - a veil covering the harsh truth of what lay beneath. Any traces of Thunder and the others were erased, swallowed up by the winter.

My heart sunk. The tracks were my tether to them, my path to follow, but now that path was lost. Yet, there was no time for despair. I had to keep moving, keep pushing.

I decided to head towards the frozen lake. That had been our original plan. We had a clear vision of the route and had communicated it to each other through the rudimentary map I had drawn in the snow. I knew Silence had understood it, and I trusted that she would do her best to stick to the plan.

Every step I took in the direction of the lake was a step into uncertainty, but I kept going. I had to keep faith, had to believe that they were out there, waiting for me on the other side of that vast, icy expanse.

With each passing hour, the landscape became more and more familiar. I recognized a tree, a rock, landmarks that told me I was on the right path.

By the time night fell, I was exhausted, my body aching from the cold and exertion. But my spirit wasn't broken. I set up a small camp, shielded from the wind by a rock outcrop, and allowed myself a moment to rest.

Tomorrow, I'll reach the lake. I don't know what I'll find there. I just hope that what awaits me is the sight of Thunder's silhouette against the horizon, the sound of Silence's laugh carried by the wind, the puppies' playful barks echoing across the ice, and Rain's familiar, comforting presence. Tomorrow, I hope to find my family.

JANUARY 11, YEAR UNKNOWN

I reached the lake today, the expanse of ice stretching before me. But the sight that awaited me was not the reunion I had envisioned. There, halfway across the lake, was the sled, sinking into the ice. My heart pounded in my chest. There was no sign of Thunder, Silence, Rain, or the puppies.

Without a second thought, I broke into a sprint towards the sinking sled. It was then that I was tackled from the side. I was sent crashing onto the ice, the breath knocked out of me. Turning, I came face to face with a monstrous undead. A heavyweight, easily 250 lbs, its grotesque, rotting features etched with insatiable hunger.

The fight was grueling, a desperate struggle for survival on the freezing ice. The zombie was powerful, but I had more at stake, more to lose. I managed to land a few solid blows, but every movement threatened to break the precarious ice underneath us.

With a final desperate heave, I managed to throw the undead off balance. It stumbled, crashing into the ice, cracking it further. In that moment, I ran. I ran for the sled, for my family, for survival.

Just as I reached the sled, the ice beneath me groaned, a hairline fracture spreading out from under my feet. I pushed off, lunging for the solid ice ahead. I landed, the momentum sliding me across the surface, away from the fractured ice.

Behind me, the ice collapsed under the weight of the undead. It plunged into the freezing water, disappearing beneath the surface. A moment of silence, then the ice resettled, closing the hole, trapping the monster beneath.

I'm safe, for now, but the sled is still sinking and there's no sign of my family. Tonight, under the moonlight reflecting off the ice, I feel a chilling loneliness that has nothing to do with the cold. Tomorrow, I'll have to continue the search. I can't lose hope. I won't.

JANUARY 12, YEAR UNKNOWN

I woke to a horrifying sight today. Hundreds of undead, lining the far side of the lake, watching. An unnatural silence fell over the frozen landscape, interrupted only by their guttural moans. For a moment, I thought they had spotted me, but their focus seemed to be on something else. Something just behind them, on the edge of the treeline to the west. As I strained my eyes to see, my heart surged. My family.

They were there, hidden among the trees, just on the edge of the zombie horde. I could see Thunder, Rain, and even the tiny forms of the puppies huddled together. And Silence... oh, how I've longed to see her safe. My heart ached at the sight, but also swelled with hope. They were alive, they were safe, but they were also trapped.

I knew then what I had to do. I had to lure the zombies away, onto the ice, and away from my family. It was a dangerous plan, but it was the only chance we had. I stepped onto the ice, carefully testing its strength. It creaked and groaned beneath me, but it held. I took a deep breath, steeled myself, and then I ran.

The undead turned as one, their sightless eyes locked on to me. I led them on a chase across the ice, their lumbering forms following me. I prayed for the ice to break beneath them, to swallow them whole.

But they were cautious, staying on the thicker ice near the shore. The lake's center, where the ice was thinnest, remained untouched. As the day came to an end, I was exhausted, cold, but not defeated. Tonight, I will rest, gather my strength, and try again tomorrow. I have to make them follow me, onto the thin ice. It's the only chance we have.

As I write this, I can still see my family in the distance, huddled in the cold, waiting for me. Tomorrow, I will get them out of there. I have to.

JANUARY 13, YEAR UNKNOWN

Today was filled with the adrenaline of a plan that I was terrified wouldn't work. My priority was to reach the sled. A morning mist shrouded the lake. It was working to my advantage. I made my way across the treacherous icy surface, my every footfall echoing in the haunting silence. Once there, I busied myself for a time with something I hoped would work, my heart pounding in my chest with a mix of fear and hope. And then, as quickly as I could, I retreated.

The undead, their eyes always watching, saw a figure on the sled, zooming towards them. The sight was irresistible for them. They lunged towards it, shambling across the ice in a grotesque parody of life. They reached the sled just as the ice began to crack beneath them. And then they saw the truth. It wasn't a human on the sled, but a decoy - a superhero mask and a blanket.

The realization was too late. The ice shattered beneath them, the freezing depths of the lake swallowing them whole. I watched as the undead disappeared beneath the ice, a sight that will haunt my dreams for days to come.

At the same time, I had skirted back to the edge of the lake, racing to my family. Our reunion was swift and filled with silent relief. We had no time for tearful greetings or joyful embraces. The danger wasn't over yet. We had to leave, to put as much distance between us and the lake as possible.

And so we did. As I write this, we are on the move once more. Today we survived. But the world out here is unforgiving. We must always be on guard, always ready for what comes next. But for tonight, I am content. We are together again. And that's all that matters.

JANUARY 14, YEAR UNKNOWN

Today was a quiet one, a welcome respite after the past few days' chaos. We took stock of our situation, assessed our supplies and planned our route forward. But throughout the day, I couldn't help but replay the events leading up to our reunion in my mind.

The others had successfully crossed the lake, the icy expanse thankfully holding up under their weight. However, their journey had not been without peril. Several undead had appeared, seemingly out of nowhere, their grotesque forms stumbling towards my family. Panicked, they had abandoned the sled, leaving it as an unintentional decoy on the frozen lake, and hidden in the treeline, out of sight.

In their fear and haste, they had not had time to take anything from the sled. Their survival instincts had kicked in and they had prioritized hiding, a choice I'm eternally grateful for. Material possessions can be replaced, lives cannot.

As the day came to an end, we gathered together for a meager meal. There was no fire, for the risk of attracting attention was too great. In the bitter cold, we huddled together for warmth, a small island of life in the vast, frozen wilderness.

As we settle down for the night, I find myself filled with a fierce determination. We have survived so much, faced so many challenges and dangers. We must keep going. For Silence, for the unborn child, for Rain and her pups, and for myself. We will face whatever this world throws at us, together.

JANUARY 15, YEAR UNKNOWN

A drone found us today. A silver fish-like creature slicing the air, its mechanical whirring slicing through the eerie silence of the wilderness. We watched it from the safety of our hiding place, its movements methodical, almost like a predator stalking its prey.

But this time, we were ready for it. Using a piece of cloth from my jacket and some rope from our supplies, we created a makeshift net. We waited for the drone to come closer, to lower itself to scan the ground, and then we sprung our trap.

The drone struggled in the net, its metal body thrashing and twisting. Silence and I rushed to the net, pulling it down with all our strength. We held the drone down, while Rain growled protectively over her pups, her ears flat against her head.

Silence worked quickly, her small hands deftly disabling the drone's systems. The struggling ceased, the whirring slowed, and then there was silence. We had captured the drone.

Our immediate thought was to destroy it, rid ourselves of the mechanical spy. But then a thought occurred to me. The drone was a link to whoever was looking for us. Could we use it to send a message? A plea for help?

As we settle in for the night, the disabled drone lying silent and still in the snow, I find myself staring at it, the moonlight glinting off its silver body. I'm filled with a strange mix of hope and dread. What will tomorrow bring, I wonder.

We'll have to wait and see.

JANUARY 16, YEAR UNKNOWN

The drone. It's been on my mind since we brought it down. The realization that we might be tracked by it has struck a nerve. Its lifeless shell lies there, a potential beacon to anyone with the ability to receive its signal. Would it lead those soldiers to us? Would they be friend or foe?

In the world before, this would have been a cause for celebration – technology aiding us, providing us with a potential line of communication. Now, it feels like a curse. I've seen enough to know that not everyone out there is looking to lend a helping hand.

Our peace, our safety – everything we've fought so hard for is threatened by this metallic harbinger. We need to make a decision. It could be our link to the outside world, our key to finding help. But it also could lead danger right to our doorstep.

We discuss it amongst ourselves. Silence is weary. I can see it in her eyes. She knows all too well the risk we run by keeping it. Yet there's a glimmer of hope in those eyes, a longing for some semblance of civilization, of normalcy. I share that hope. But there's a decision to be made and it's not an easy one.

As we tuck in for the night, the drone lies buried under a heap of snow. Out of sight, out of mind, for now. But we can't ignore it for long. Tomorrow, we'll need to decide our next course of action. For now, we rest with the knowledge that our quiet existence could be upended any moment. The anxiety is palpable, the silence deafening.

Tomorrow, we decide our fate.

JANUARY 17, YEAR UNKNOWN

I woke up today with a grim determination, the sound of the gunships in the distance a stark reminder of our perilous existence. There is a gnawing sensation in my gut, a sense of urgency I haven't felt since the world collapsed around me. The drone, our unwanted gift, had to go.

I loaded the drone onto Thunder's back, bidding a silent goodbye to Silence and the pups, each tucked away in their makeshift bed, Rain sitting faithfully beside them. I hoped this would be the last they saw of this cursed piece of technology.

With the drone on Thunder, I set off into the early dawn, the silence of the landscape punctuated by the distant sound of gunships. The cold wind howled around me, but I felt a calm resolve. This was my task, my responsibility, and I would see it through.

I made my way deeper into the wasteland, the drone growing heavier with every step. It was a strange feeling, as if I was riding away from our fragile peace and back into the chaos we had escaped.

As I reached what I felt was a safe distance, I disassembled the drone carefully, scattering its parts across the desolate landscape. The drone, once a silent observer, was now nothing more than scrap. I looked at the pieces scattered around, a symbol of a world that once was, now buried in the frozen tundra.

I headed back, my heart heavy but my spirit light. As I saw the distant silhouettes of Silence, Rain, and the pups, I knew I had made the right decision. The threat was gone, for now. But the question remained – how long until our past catches up with us again? Only time would tell. For now, we could breathe a sigh of relief.

JANUARY 18, YEAR UNKNOWN

An unexpected encounter today has left me on high alert. A group of survivors, haggard and gaunt, stumbled upon our encampment this afternoon. They claimed to have been wandering the desolate landscapes for days, famished and exhausted. Despite their apparent innocence, there was something about them that set me on edge.

Their reactions to my appearance were oddly subdued. Even Thunder's imposing presence seemed to elicit less surprise than I had expected. This lack of shock, combined with the desperate glint in their eyes, raised a silent alarm in my mind. In this brutal world, it was never wise to trust too easily.

Silence and I decided to provide them with some food and water, but we remained wary. Despite their thankfulness, I couldn't shake off my unease. I caught them exchanging glances, their eyes sweeping over our camp, taking in our resources, our defenses. Their leader, a man named Jonah, was particularly insistent on knowing where we were headed.

I felt the tension thicken with each passing hour, their presence an intrusion on the relative peace we had established. But as night fell, I felt a creeping dread. It was becoming apparent that these survivors weren't as harmless as they first appeared.

As I sit here, penning this entry in the dim glow of our campfire, I find my hand instinctively resting on the hilt of my blade. Every rustle, every whisper from their direction sets my nerves on edge. I only hope my instincts are wrong, that these are just weary souls seeking shelter.

Tonight, I will sleep with one eye open, ready for whatever may come. Tomorrow, we need to find a way to deal with this. The safety of Silence, Rain, and the pups is my priority. Their well-being, their survival is all that matters.

JANUARY 19, YEAR UNKNOWN

In the stealth of the night, we attempted to leave. My fears had manifested, and I couldn't ignore the unsettling feeling that our lives were in danger. Silently, we started packing, careful not to rouse suspicion. But despite our caution, our movements were detected.

As the chilling wind whistled through the skeletal trees, their leader, Jonah, emerged from the shadows. His face, previously masked by a veneer of friendliness, was now hardened and cold. He gestured for his men to surround us. The air was thick with menace as they closed in, their eyes reflecting the grim moonlight.

They didn't say a word. There were no threats, no demands. We were held captive by an invisible chain, the palpable tension tying us to them. It felt as though we were being kept for someone or something, as if we were just pieces in a bigger game. I watched them cautiously, my every instinct screaming that danger was looming.

Silence clutched my arm tightly, her eyes wide with fear. I gave her a reassuring squeeze, trying to convey that I wouldn't let anything happen to her. Rain growled lowly, her protective instincts flaring. The pups huddled close to their mother, too young to understand the gravity of the situation but aware enough to sense the threat.

As dawn approached, we were still trapped in this silent standoff. Our captors gave no indication of their intentions. My mind raced, contemplating our next move. I could only hope that whatever or whoever they were waiting for would arrive soon, and that we would find a way to escape unscathed. But as the first light of day pierced the dense cloud cover, my hope was waning. We were trapped in a game of waiting and uncertainty.

JANUARY 20, YEAR UNKNOWN

Today was a grueling test of patience. With the hostage situation hanging over us like a dark cloud, every tick of the clock felt like a crushing weight.

Jonah and his men kept their distance, watching us with predatory eyes. Their silent vigilance was unnerving, a constant reminder of the tight leash they had us on.

The idea of unleashing my rage upon them flirted with my thoughts. The beast within yearned for a release, to protect its pack at any cost. But rationality tamed the beast. I knew I couldn't risk it. The possibility of not taking them all out before they harmed Silence... it was a gamble I wasn't willing to make.

So, we played nice. We waited. We sat around a dying fire, Silence and I sharing hushed conversations. We spoke of mundane things, of past joys, of simpler times. We laughed at old jokes, told stories to the pups. We were attempting to create a bubble of normality, a shield against the tense atmosphere around us.

But underneath it all, a coil of anxiety wound tighter with each passing hour. I couldn't help but let my mind wander to what awaited us. Who were they waiting for? What were their plans? The dread was a bitter pill, hard to swallow.

As night fell, the cold set in. We huddled together for warmth, our bodies creating a living barrier against the icy wind. The enemy was just shadows in the darkness, their silent forms ominous in the dim light. We waited, the anticipation a cruel torment. And all I could do was hold Silence close, reassuring her that whatever comes next, we would face it together.

JANUARY 21, YEAR UNKNOWN

Today dawned with the droning echo of helicopter blades beating against the morning sky. Jonah's men tensed up, their eyes gleaming with anticipation as they watched the military chopper descend from the heavens.

As the dust cleared, a squadron of uniformed figures emerged, their grim expressions masked behind dark visors. They pointed at me, issuing a command that cut through the chilly morning air, "You, come with us." I bared my teeth, every fiber in me ready to pounce, ready to make them regret their audacity.

But then, they laid a hand on Silence. Just a touch, but it was enough to ignite a primal rage within me. I was ready to unleash hell on them when I saw Silence nod at me. Her eyes were calm, resolute. She was telling me to go, and I saw in her gaze a trust, a belief that we would meet again.

As they shackled me, leading me towards the chopper, I could feel Thunder's wild agitation. He bucked and reared, letting out sharp whinnies of protest. The soldiers tried to restrain him, but Thunder was a force of nature. He refused to be tamed. As the chopper lifted off, carrying me away from my family, Thunder dashed underneath, his wild eyes tracking me.

As we rose higher and higher, I watched them grow smaller. Silence, the pups, Rain, all huddled together, surrounded by men whose intentions I did not know. Thunder, circling wildly below us, refusing to be separated from his pack. It was a sight that tore at my heart, filling me with a sense of dread and helplessness I had never known before.

But as the chopper whisked me away, my mind wasn't focused on the chains binding me or the unknown fate awaiting me. It was on them, my family, their faces etched into my mind's eye, their safety my only concern. This was far from over, and I vowed to do whatever it takes to return to them.

JANUARY 22, YEAR UNKNOWN

The familiar hum of fluorescent lights is a stark contrast to the stillness of the wild. I'm surrounded by bare walls, cold metal, and a small cot - my current universe. It is an alien, claustrophobic space compared to the open world I've known for years.

The room is secure - locks on the outside, no windows, but it doesn't reek of menace. Rather, it feels like a protective measure, a barrier between the raw, dangerous creature they perceive me to be, and the world they're trying to protect. I don't feel in danger here; rather, I feel a deep concern for Silence, Rain, and the pups.

These are military people - stern, disciplined, focused. I don't see hostility in their eyes when they slide meals through the slot in the door, just caution. The meals themselves are a luxury, canned food with a variety I haven't tasted in years. Yet, it's hard to enjoy it while my mind is constantly drawn back to my family.

They must've kept an eye on me for a while. How else would they know about my connection to Silence, how else would they have guessed to use her as leverage to get me on the chopper? I just hope they didn't do anything foolish after I left.

For now, all I can do is bide my time. They have questions, I know, and maybe, just maybe, they have answers too. Perhaps, for all the anxiety clawing at me, this is the opportunity we've been seeking, the chance to find the cure.

I keep reminding myself - I'm here for Silence, for the child, for Rain and the pups. I'm here so we might all have a chance at a normal life again. As night falls, I hold on to that thought, finding a sense of calm in the uncertain silence. Tomorrow, I'll face whatever comes my way. For them.

JANUARY 23, YEAR UNKNOWN

The door swings open and in steps a man, worn by age and a life spent in the harsh reality of this world. He carries himself with a certain authority, an air of command. His eyes meet mine and there's a spark, a flicker of recognition. He knows me, or at least, he knew me once.

"Sergeant," he greets, a note of respect in his voice. But he doesn't call me Lance. To him, I am a soldier.

He speaks with caution, as if unsure how to navigate a conversation with the undead. Despite the grim circumstances, it almost brings a smirk to my lips. If only he knew how long I've spent trying to recall the echoes of my past, trying to reconcile the man I was with the creature I've become.

He's here to negotiate. He tells me that he can help, that there's hope. But his assistance comes at a cost. I am to aid them, to lend them the strength that this cursed existence has granted me. I brush him off. My mind is filled only with thoughts of Silence, Rain, the pups. Where are they? Are they safe?

When I ask about my family, his features harden. The veneer of camaraderie slips, replaced by a darker, more sinister air. His words are a veiled threat, a pointed reminder of the power they hold over me.

"Without our help, Sergeant," he says, "there's no telling when you'll see your family again, or in what condition you'll find them."

He seems to mistake my silent rage as an invitation to bore me to death and introduces himself as General Frederick Maddox. Maddox had always been a man who lived in the shadow of his father, a decorated military man renowned for his heroism and integrity. Growing up, Maddox was constantly reminded of the greatness he was expected to achieve, of the legacy he was meant to continue.

This unending pressure pushed Maddox into the military at a young age. He was a natural leader, charismatic and cunning, with a knack for strategy that helped him quickly rise through the ranks. But for all his achievements, he always felt overshadowed by the memory of his father. It wasn't enough for him to be just as good; he had to be better.

When the outbreak hit, Maddox saw an opportunity. Here was a crisis unlike any the world had ever seen, a threat that could decimate the human race. And he, General Frederick Maddox, would be the one to save humanity. He saw it as his destiny, his chance to finally step out of his father's shadow and make his mark on the world.

But somewhere along the way, it seemed Maddox lost sight of his initial purpose. He became obsessed with the idea of harnessing the power of the curse. He began conducting experiments, pushing the boundaries of morality and humanity in his quest for power. He convinced himself that the end justified the means. He waited for some reaction, something from me. I had nothing. He is irrelevant to me. A noise.

He leaves then, leaving me alone with my thoughts, flashes of recognition in the red mist that has descended upon me. I am no stranger to this danger, but the safety of my family is a weakness they've exploited without hesitation. It's a blow, and it stings more than any wound I've suffered.

Night falls, and I sit in the silence, a sense of dread seeping into my bones. What choice do I have but to play their game? The lives of those I hold dear hang in the balance.

Yet, amidst the fear, a seed of resolve takes root. They want my help. They need me. And maybe, just maybe, that gives me the upper hand.

I have a long night ahead to think, to strategize. I am Lance, I am a soldier, and I will fight. For Silence, for Rain, for the little ones. For us.

JANUARY 24, YEAR UNKNOWN

The decision has been made. It's a matter of survival, a choice that is not a choice at all. I agree to their terms, to their twisted pact. But as I walk these sterile halls, guided by uniformed shadows, my mind is at work.

A bespectacled man, with the sickly aroma of fresh vanilla takes me on a tour, shows me their fortress of steel and concrete. This is a military operation, a hive buzzing with activity. The facility is sprawling, an intimidating expanse of rooms and corridors, of high-tech labs and holding cells. Each area guarded by coded doors, the codes concealed but not enough to evade my watchful gaze. I commit them to memory, every detail I hope to salvage from the fog of my mind.

They see me shuffle, see my gaze wander, and they think they've fooled me. They believe they're in control, that they've tamed the monster. I let them. I have to. But with each passing moment, each calculated act of submissiveness, I am preparing. I am observing. And I am waiting.

Finally, Vanilla brings me to my quarters. A watchtower room overlooking the expanse of the compound. It's a cage with a view, a subtle reminder of the freedom that lies just beyond my reach. This is where I'm to stay, where I'm to await my mission briefing.

The door closes behind me, the lock clicks into place, and I am alone once more. The sickly sweet smell lingers and I notice him still watching me, smiling. And then he's finally gone. He whistles a tune as he goes. I move to the window, my eyes tracing the lines of the facility, the cold expanse beyond it. The loneliness stings, but it fuels my determination.

Each echo of my past life that resurfaces, every piece of the soldier I once was, strengthens my resolve. I will play their game. I will be the soldier they need. But in the end, it is not for them.

It's for Silence. For Rain. For the pups. For us. I will remember. I will fight. I will bring us back together. And if it's the last thing I do, I will make them pay for ripping us apart.

JANUARY 25, YEAR UNKNOWN

The mission briefing brings a fresh wave of bitter reality. This military operation, their solution to reclaim what's been lost, is all a game of pawns. And I am their pawn, chosen to infiltrate a survivor camp up on a mountain. It seems this stronghold has in its possession a vital resource - an electronic briefcase, apparently lost during a medical chopper accident. This briefcase contains something of paramount importance - the core vials of the cure template. These vials are what everyone has been fighting for - the potential key to undoing the undeath that has taken over the world.

Their choppers can't reach the camp because of the thin mountain air, their tanks can't traverse the steep ground, and their soldiers are deemed too "normal" to get past the "evolved" survivors guarding their prize. I'm their best bet. A half-undead, half-human soldier who doesn't sleep, doesn't need to breathe as much, and can take a bullet without batting an eyelid. The hope is that my unique 'abilities' will see me through, will allow me to complete this mission successfully.

The magnitude of the mission weighs heavily on me. But if this is what it takes to get back to my family, to Silence, Rain and the pups... then so be it. The mountain waits, and with it, my new mission. The key to the cure, the key to my past, and the key to my future.

JANUARY 27, YEAR UNKNOWN

As the last rays of the sun fade behind the mountain, I find myself standing at its foot, a silhouette looming against the darkening sky. It's a sight that is both unfamiliar yet vaguely recognizable. I realize with a jolt of mixed emotions that I'm seeing a mirror image of the mountain that my family and I were navigating around. If they're still where we parted, they're on the other side. It's a thought that twists my gut with worry, but I push it down. I must focus on the task at hand.

The personnel leave, their duty fulfilled in dropping me off at this godforsaken place. They leave me with a singular weapon - a long blade with a hefty grip, designed for one-handed usage. It doesn't require bullets or delicate finger work, won't run out of ammunition, and most importantly, it's silent.

JANUARY 28, YEAR UNKNOWN

The climb is grueling, a test of will and determination. But I do not falter. Every step brings me closer to the objective, every silent breath is a testament to my resolve. The thinning air doesn't bother me as it would a human. The chill of the night is only a faint reminder of the living man I once was. It's a benefit, perhaps the only one, of my undead condition.

The moonlight provides enough light for me to see the terrain. I navigate through the craggy rocks and patches of thinning snow, the silence around me broken only by the soft crunch of my boots. The silence is unnerving, eerie, like the calm before a storm. I can't help but anticipate the danger lurking nearby.

I arrive at the outskirts of the survivor camp by midnight. The flickering light of a distant fire paints dancing shadows on the mountain wall. I stay hidden, studying the camp, watching for guards, listening for the rhythm of the camp's life. I don't see the briefcase, but I didn't expect to. It's there, somewhere, hidden just like me. I pull the blade a little closer, ready for the night ahead.

JANUARY 29, YEAR UNKNOWN

As I approached the camp in the darkness, I felt a cold unease that had little to do with the frigid air. As I slipped into their camp, I found them ready for me, their guns pointed in my direction. There was no time for thoughts, only action.

They opened fire immediately, the sounds of their weapons echoing off the cliffs. It was a hailstorm of bullets, and I was caught in the middle. I charged forward, a snarl tearing itself from my throat. The survivors scattered, their screams and curses filling the air. They fought, but their weapons were useless against the beast I'd become.

It took every last ounce of my strength, every bit of my inhuman resilience, to fight my way past them and into the cave where they kept their valuables. I found the briefcase among the treasures they had gathered, a beacon of hope in the midst of death and destruction.

As I emerged from the cave, the camp was eerily quiet. Bodies lay scattered in the snow, the result of my violent intrusion. I retrieved the briefcase and began the treacherous descent down the mountain.

As the adrenaline drained from my body, the reality of what I had done hit me hard. I felt a chill of dread that surpassed the biting cold.

There, by the stream, I saw a young child - a zombie like me. It was alone, its wide, frightened eyes watching me. The realization hit me like a punch to the gut - I had just annihilated this child's protectors, its family.

I wanted to explain, to say that I had no choice, but the words wouldn't come. Instead, the child reached out and placed a comforting hand on my arm, its touch surprisingly gentle. I felt my heart twist at the gesture.

That night, I did something I hadn't done in a long time. I cried. Not for the pain of my wounds, but for the guilt and the horror of what I'd done.

Something changed in me on that mountain. I was no longer just a soldier, a survivor. I was a monster, a weapon used to enact someone else's will.

As the night drew to a close, I found myself haunted by the memory of the child's touch, its innocence, its trust. It was a stark reminder of the world I'd lost, and the monster I'd become.

JANUARY 30, YEAR UNKNOWN

One of the darkest days of my new life. The drones came first, buzzing overhead, their cameras taking in the carnage I'd caused. And then the helicopter arrived, bringing with it the cold, impersonal efficiency of the military.

As I approached them, weighed down by guilt and regret, the zombie child ran towards the helicopter, its arms outstretched, curious. What happened next will haunt me until my final breath. The crack of a gunshot echoed through the mountains, and the child dropped to the ground, headless. Vanilla licked his lips, and hopped down from the chopper.

I felt something inside me snap. I roared, a sound of pure grief and fury, and lunged towards them. But they were ready for me. A sniper's bullet caught me in the chest, sending me crashing back into the snow. The last thing I remember is watching them retrieve the briefcase, their gloved hands handling it with almost reverent care.

When I woke up, I was alone. The helicopters were gone, the briefcase was gone. The only sign that they'd ever been there was the body of the child, its eyes still open and staring blankly at the sky.

I found the vials in my sling, a cruel reminder of my mission. I knew what I had to do. I needed to get these vials to safety, to find my family, and then to disappear. I couldn't let them find me, couldn't let them use me like this again.

I gathered my strength and started the long journey down the mountain. I knew that I had to hide, had to protect myself and the vials at all costs. But first, I had to find my family. I had to make sure they were safe. And then, I had to fight.

JANUARY 31, YEAR UNKNOWN

A blizzard. Everything seems impossible. Head is pain. Restlessly resting.

FEBRUARY 1, YEAR UNKNOWN

Trudging again through the heavy blizzard, I stumbled upon the place where I had hidden the remnants of the drone. The snow had done a good job of preserving the machine, and despite the freezing cold numbing my fingers, I managed to piece it back together.

There was a part of me, a human part, that hesitated. This machine represented those who had used me, manipulated me into causing unimaginable pain. But there was also the part of me that knew that the drone could prove useful. It could be a tool, a weapon, or even a means to find my family.

So, with the drone safely tucked into my bag and the vials secured against my chest, I continued my journey through the merciless snowstorm. Every step was a battle against the biting cold, against the nagging doubt, against the haunting memories.

But I had something to fight for now - a purpose that went beyond mere survival. I had to keep the vials safe. I had to find my family. I had to make things right.

FEBRUARY 2, YEAR UNKNOWN

The biting cold seemed to have become a constant companion now. The endless expanse of white stretched in all directions, reflecting the bright sunlight and painting a picture of desolate beauty. My footsteps were the only disturbances in the immaculate canvas of snow.

In the far distance, I heard the sound of a helicopter, faint but growing steadily louder. I quickly found a nook in the snowy landscape to hide. There, I lay silently, watching the chopper cross the sky. It felt like an ominous reminder of the dangers that still lurked, waiting for a moment of weakness.

Later, I came across a frozen stream. The ice was so clear that I could see the rocks at the bottom, locked away under the glassy surface. It was eerily beautiful, yet its sight filled me with an inexplicable sadness.

As I sat there, resting my weary body and mind, I found myself wandering back to a time before all this. A time when a stream wasn't just a potential water source or a possible threat, but an invitation to splash, play, and laugh without care. A time when laughter wasn't a rarity.

Life was different then. Simpler, perhaps. But that was a past life, and I am a different creature now. However, the memories of that past life and the hope for a safer future for my makeshift family were what kept me pushing forward. With renewed determination, I continued my journey into the unknown.

FEBRUARY 3, YEAR UNKNOWN

Today, I stumbled upon an unnerving spectacle: a field full of crows. They blanketed the ground, thousands of them, their jet-black feathers standing out starkly against the snow. They watched me pass with beady eyes, a mass of silent observers. The only sound was the soft rustle of their wings and their occasional, quiet cawing. It was as though the world itself had hushed to respect their presence.

The sight of such a large gathering of these carrion birds filled me with dread. In the old world, a field of crows was seen as an omen of death. And now? In a world already overrun by death, their presence seemed to hold an even more ominous significance.

Even so, I moved carefully through the crow field, making sure not to startle them into flight. I didn't want to attract any unwanted attention.

As the last crow faded from my view, their collective gaze still seemed to bore into my back, a haunting reminder of the danger I was in, the perilous mission I had undertaken. Their silent judgment was an eerie end to another day of survival.

FEBRUARY 4, YEAR UNKNOWN

In the early morning, a discovery: hoof tracks in the snow. Thunder's tracks. They are fresh, the edges sharp and clear in the powdery snow. My heart lifts at the sight - my loyal companion is nearby. Or at least he was, recently.

I follow the tracks, my senses alert. The dread of the crow field lingers, but there is a new hope stirring within me. The hoof prints are my guide, leading me through the barren landscape, and with each step, I grow more certain that I will soon see my family again.

But there is a tension in the air, an ominous stillness that gives me pause. The world around me seems to hold its breath, the landscape stretched taut with anticipation. The memories of the assault on the mountain, the killing, the child, they are a heavy weight in my heart, a constant reminder of the consequences of my actions.

The day ends with no sign of Thunder, just the silent whisper of his tracks leading me onward, through the snow, into the unknown.

FEBRUARY 5, YEAR UNKNOWN

I had an encounter today, one that felt eerily familiar. I found an injured zombie wolf, its hind leg twisted in an unnatural way. I remembered Whisky, and how our first meeting was under similar circumstances. My heart ached at the memory.

This time though, there was a difference. The wolf was terrified of me. It snarled and whimpered, cowering back from me as I approached. The smell of decay and infection was strong, a grotesque parody of the living creature it once was.

I did what I could for it. I straightened its leg, setting the bone as best as I could, though I knew it would never truly heal. I gave it some of the meat I had scavenged, and it ate ravenously, its yellowed eyes watching me warily all the while.

When I left, it did not follow. It lay there, in the snow, its ragged breaths filling the silence of the frozen landscape. I don't know if it will survive, but I had to try. After all, I am not so different from it, a creature out of place in this world, simply trying to survive.

The rest of the day passed in a blur of white, the snowfall making it hard to follow Thunder's tracks. As night fell, I found myself hoping that the wolf would find some measure of peace, just as I hope to find my family soon.

FEBRUARY 6, YEAR UNKNOWN

There was danger today, close and persistent. I spent most of the day hiding, crouching behind rocks and trees, my body still and silent. The danger? It came in the form of heavy armored vehicles moving slowly and ominously through the landscape, their engines rumbling in a disturbing rhythm that echoed off the mountainside. I recognized them as military, the same ones who had taken me, used me, and left me for dead.

My heart pounded in my chest like a drum, and I could feel the vibrations of the vehicles even from my hidden spot. I didn't dare move, for fear they'd spot me. The hum of the engines continued for what felt like hours, each minute dragging out into an eternity.

The vehicles finally moved on, leaving nothing but disturbed snow and silence in their wake. I resumed my journey, my footsteps careful and quiet. I felt like a ghost, moving through a world that was at once familiar and alien. The military presence confirmed my fears - they're still searching, probably for me and the vials I've stolen.

As night fell, I found a secluded spot to rest, my mind racing with thoughts and worries. I know now that I must be careful, must stay hidden, must move quietly and cautiously. The road to find my family has become even more perilous, and I can't afford to make any mistakes.

I am alone, a creature of the night, navigating through a landscape that feels more hostile than ever. But I will not be deterred. I will find my family. I must.

FEBRUARY 7, YEAR UNKNOWN

The day started like any other - cold, silent, and filled with an endless expanse of white snow. My journey took me further through the wilderness, each step taking me closer to an unknown destination. I was walking aimlessly when I saw a thin plume of smoke reaching up into the sky in the distance. It was a beacon of hope in this desolate landscape.

I approached cautiously, the harsh lessons of the past days still fresh in my mind. But as I neared, my senses started to pick up familiar scents. The unmistakable scent of Thunder, the faint trace of Silence, and Rain... My heart pounded as the realization hit me. They had been here. My family. They were close. I could feel it.

The camp was recently deserted when I arrived. The fire was still smoldering, and there were clear signs of a quick departure. An uneaten meal, still warm, sat in a pot over the fire. Footprints, both human and animal, led away from the camp, disappearing into the snow-covered landscape.

But they had been here, and recently. That gave me a renewed sense of hope. They were alive, and they were close.

As night fell, I settled into the deserted camp, the remnants of their presence comforting me. I can't shake off the feeling that I am close, so close to finding them. I need to believe that. As the cold seeped in, I huddled closer to the dying embers of the fire, my thoughts occupied with my family.

Tonight, I sleep with a sense of hope, a feeling I thought I'd forgotten. I am closer to my family, and tomorrow, I will continue my journey.

FEBRUARY 8, YEAR UNKNOWN

A hushed silence fills the air today as my thoughts wander back to that old documentary film reel and the "place of salvation". The memory of it has a bitter taste now. The lofty ideals it portrayed, the promise of salvation, seems more like an illusion. I've seen the reality, the military, the shadowy organization that claimed to be our salvation. They were nothing more than a misguided group, and their flaws were glaringly obvious.

The vials I carry seem to weigh heavier with each passing day. The supposed "cure" templates are a testament to their flawed ideals and their misplaced hopes. I can't help but question their intentions, their truth. What is the real purpose of these vials? Do they hold a cure, a weapon, or something else entirely?

And if they are as important as they claimed, why were they so readily abandoned after a mere accident? It doesn't add up. Nothing about this does. They seemed eager to recover them but not for the reasons they claimed. There's something else, something they aren't telling me.

The military men I encountered were far from the beacon of hope the documentary had promised. Their incompetence was apparent, their actions rash and thoughtless. They had no qualms about shooting down a child, abandoning me to die. I've been used as a pawn, manipulated, betrayed.

As I sit in the silence of the abandoned camp, my doubts and thoughts swim around me. The reality of my situation is becoming clearer, and it's far from the salvation I was led to believe. But despite everything, I still hold on to a glimmer of hope. I need to find my family, protect them, and perhaps, find our own salvation.

Tomorrow, I continue my journey, but tonight, I rest with my doubts and fears. I just hope I can find the strength to carry on when dawn breaks.

FEBRUARY 9, YEAR UNKNOWN

The world is a stark contrast to what it once was. The colors of humanity have faded into a dreary white, the constant snowfall shrouding the remnants of civilization. It has been nearly a fortnight since the incident on the mountain, and each day I find myself missing my family more. The ache in my chest is unrelenting, a physical manifestation of the void their absence has left.

I continue to trudge forward, hoping to pick up their trail once again. But the biting cold, the near-constant snowfall, and the omnipresent threat of human pursuers make each step an ordeal. Every night, I hunker down in makeshift shelters, listening to the whisper of the wind and the distant cries of the undead. Sleep is elusive, but I force myself to rest, to recover as much as I can.

The drone, disassembled and tucked away in my pack, serves as a constant reminder of the danger that nips at my heels. I'm aware of the risk it carries, the beacon it could potentially be for my pursuers. Yet, there is also a potential advantage – a tool I might be able to use in a desperate situation. Perhaps there are still frequencies it could tap into, messages it could intercept.

The briefcase – the damned briefcase. Questions plague me about the vials. Are they real? A cure? If so, what does the military intend for it? And why was it lost so carelessly?

I'm tired, more tired than I've ever been. But I press on. There is no other option. I need to find my family. I need to keep them safe. I need to unravel the truth of this cure. My past, my present, and my uncertain future are intertwined in this quest. I pray that I'll have the strength to see it through.

The long night falls, wrapping the world in its icy embrace. I huddle into my makeshift shelter, clutching the briefcase closer. Tomorrow, I press on. Tomorrow, I get closer to my family.

FEBRUARY 10, YEAR UNKNOWN

In the depth of the chilling morning, I continue my journey, the path before me obscured by fresh layers of snow. Anticipation hangs in the air as I navigate through the snow-covered wilderness.

By midday, I stumble upon a clearing with fresh tracks. My heart freezes for a moment - the mark of a boot, a child's shoe imprint, sled tracks, and the unmistakable hooves of Thunder. It's them.

I follow the tracks, each step igniting the spark of hope that had kept me moving forward. And there, amidst a sheltering grove of evergreens, I find them. My family.

Silence, Thunder, Rain and her pups - they're all there. Surprise and relief wash over their faces as I step into their sight. Silence rushes to me, throwing her arms around me in a tight hug. The joy in Thunder's eyes mirrors my own relief as he greets me with a shake of his head and a playful snort. Rain's tail wags vigorously, the pups tumbling over each other in their excitement.

This reunion, saturated with relief and happiness, is a balm to the wounds of our separation. Yes, the world outside our circle is still treacherous, but this moment of unity gives us strength. We've endured so much, survived when the odds were stacked against us. Now, we stand together again, ready to face what lies ahead.

As I remove my pack, I feel the weight of the vials, an ominous reminder of the mission I've agreed to undertake. I decide to keep them hidden for now, unspoken in the midst of our reunion. Today, we relish in being a family once more, taking solace in our shared strength. Whatever the future holds, we'll face it together.

FEBRUARY 11, YEAR UNKNOWN

I should have seen it coming, the signs were there. As we walked, Silence fell behind. She was usually so steady, so strong. But not today. Her breath came in short, ragged gasps. And then she couldn't go any further.

Silence was in labor.

It was not a good place to give birth, exposed and far from shelter, but we didn't have a choice. I cleared the snow around us as best I could, making a makeshift nest for Silence. The others, Rain and her pups, huddled close, providing warmth and protection.

It was a long, arduous process. Silence was strong, stronger than any of us. But even she couldn't hide the pain. Finally, as the sun started to set, we heard the cries of a new life. Silence had given birth to a baby girl.

She was small, fragile, like any newborn. Her cries echoed in the frozen wilderness, a symbol of life amidst so much death.

We couldn't stay there, in the open. As soon as Silence was able to move, we started off again. I carried the baby, swaddled in layers of clothing, in my sling. We walked, under the light of the moon, with the sounds of the newborn's gentle breaths as our guiding soundtrack.

The world is harsh, dangerous. We've already lost Whisky, and who knows what more we will have to endure. But for now, we have a new life. A small flicker of hope in this desolate landscape. And we will do whatever it takes to keep her safe.

FEBRUARY 12, YEAR UNKNOWN

In the snow-blanketed wilderness, our tired eyes found a small beacon of hope. An old cabin, partially visible and half-buried by an avalanche. Its windows were dark, as were the surrounding woods. We approached it carefully, weary but hopeful.

The door was buried under the snow. With some effort, I cleared it enough to force it open. It was eerie inside, the lingering silence heavy with stories of those who might have once called it home.

It was not much but it was shelter, a rarity in these forsaken times. We huddled together, kindling a small fire from the remnants of furniture. The warmth was a welcome respite against the relentless cold outside.

Silence lay with the newborn on the only remaining bed, a tired but satisfied smile on her face. Rain and her pups settled near the fire, their eyes heavy with exhaustion.

I spent the night reinforcing the cabin's frail structure as best as I could, using bits of old furniture and whatever else I could find. I knew we couldn't stay here indefinitely, but for now, it was a haven for us, for Silence and her baby.

When dawn came, I looked out at the vast expanse of snow, the vials heavy in my sling. The world outside was still as cold, still as deadly. But inside our little haven, there was life. A tiny spark of it, flickering stubbornly in the darkness.

As I watched Silence and the newborn sleep, I realized that this was what we were fighting for. A chance to live, a chance to see another day. A chance to create small pockets of warmth in a world that had grown so cold.

We are still far from safe, but for now, we have a home. A place to rest, a place to breathe. And I intend to do whatever it takes to protect it.

FEBRUARY 13, YEAR UNKNOWN

Yesterday was a strange one. It was tranquil, serene, almost peaceful. In the midst of the desolation that our world has become, we found joy.

Thunder spent the day outside, running through the thick blankets of snow, his mane flowing in the wind. His joy was palpable, infectious. It's hard to imagine that this formidable beast who has seen so much was once a gentle creature, devoid of any aggression. I watched him from the window, his heavy frame a stark contrast against the white landscape.

Inside the cabin, we took turns holding the newborn. She's so tiny, so delicate. I can hardly believe that she came into this world, that she exists at all. Yet here she is, a testament to the indomitable human spirit, an emblem of hope amidst despair.

Silence is a pillar of strength. She cooed and hummed gently to the baby, her face filled with a love so profound it filled the room. She has taken to motherhood as if it was always meant for her. Perhaps it was. Despite everything, she radiates a calmness, a tranquility that eases our anxieties.

Even Rain and her pups were not immune to the joy. They spent the day in a happy stupor, lazily napping by the fire.

The cabin felt warmer, felt more like a home than any place has in a long time. For once, we had a moment of respite from our grim reality. It was a day filled with joy. A day when we forgot about the monsters that lurk outside. A day when we were just a family, living in our little home, surrounded by snow and silence.

The vials in my sling felt a little less heavy. I know that we can't stay hidden forever, but for now, we are safe. We are together. And that's all that matters.

FEBRUARY 14, YEAR UNKNOWN

Something unusual is happening with Rain's pups. Their development is on fast forward, accelerating at a rate that seems unnatural, and it's become impossible to ignore. They opened their eyes days sooner than expected. They began walking around, albeit clumsily, after just a week. And now, they've started eating solid food. They're maturing rapidly, displaying a level of understanding and awareness that seems beyond their age.

I have my theories, although none of them are entirely comforting. Rain was a zombie for a while, before I donated my antidote. Perhaps that has altered her in some fundamental way, which in turn, has affected her pups. Or perhaps it is my blood coursing through their veins, having been passed on from their mother, which is causing this unusual growth.

Regardless of the cause, these are uncharted waters. As a curious man in my past life, I would have found this intriguing, a scientific mystery to be unraveled. But now, the stakes are too high. These pups are not just subjects in a grand experiment, they're part of our family.

What does this accelerated growth mean for them? Will they grow old before their time? Or have they inherited some kind of super strength, an ability to withstand the virus, or worse, become carriers of a new strain? There's a looming cloud of uncertainty, and it's growing darker with each passing day.

For now, all I can do is observe, keep them safe and healthy, and hope that whatever is happening, is for the best. I have no other choice.

FEBRUARY 15, YEAR UNKNOWN

A shrill beeping sound breaks the silence of the cabin. My heart pounds against my chest as I pull the bag closer and rip it open. The drone. It's making that noise. But why now? Did it somehow reactivate itself?

Silence's eyes widen with worry. The pups whimper, huddling closer to Rain. I scramble to the drone, fumbling with the pieces as I try to remember how to disarm it. It's a dance of my fingers over cold metal, my mind racing through each wire and part.

Finally, the beeping stops. I sit back, the drone in my hands silent once more, but the fear still lingers. We've disarmed it, but the damage might already be done. Could it have sent out a signal? Were our coordinates now flashing across some military screen? We thought we were safe in this hidden cabin, cocooned by the snow, but were we just fooling ourselves? I curse my foggy mind. The unexpected birth had distracted me even further and my plan to use the drone had backfired in the worst possible way.

There are no easy answers, just the weight of uncertainty pressing down on us. We're in the dark, both figuratively and literally, as the sun dips below the horizon. There's an eerie quietness that hangs in the cabin, as we listen intently for any sounds that would signal an incoming threat.

We decide to stay put for the night, bolstering our defences as best we can. I bury the drone in the snow once again, far from the cabin, hopefully out of reach from any prying signals. There's a shift in the air, a sense of danger lurking just beyond our door. The peaceful days we'd experienced now feel like a dream, a calm before the storm.

All we can do is prepare... and wait.

FEBRUARY 16, YEAR UNKNOWN

The morning sun paints the world in a cold, white light. The night passed without incident, but the peaceful morning does little to quell our unease. The constant, gnawing worry that we've been found is impossible to shake off. We make the unanimous decision - it's time to move on.

Packing our few belongings takes no time at all. I take one last look around the cabin that had been our home for a few days. It offered us shelter and comfort, but now, it feels tainted, its safety compromised by our fears.

Silence is quiet, her face pale but determined. She cradles the pups in her arms, who are blissfully unaware of the danger we may be in. Rain sticks close to her, a protective mother through and through.

Thunder seems to understand the gravity of the situation, his usually playful demeanor replaced with seriousness. His gaze meets mine, a silent promise that he will protect us all. I pat his strong neck, drawing strength from his unwavering loyalty.

We set out, leaving the cabin behind. The snow crunches under our feet, the only sound in the otherwise silent wilderness. There's a certain cold finality to our departure, a forced farewell to a place we had begun to consider home.

But survival isn't about comfort or settling down, it's about adapting, moving, living to fight another day. And so, we press on, carrying our fears and hopes with us into the unknown.

FEBRUARY 17, YEAR UNKNOWN

The farther we move away from the mountain region, the less we hear the distant rumble of engines. A haunting silence gradually replaces the mechanical roars, broken only by the crunch of our boots against the snowy ground. The harsh mountain winds have given way to calmer breezes, whistling through the barren trees and rustling the frozen grass under our feet.

We trudge through snow-blanketed fields and winding forest paths, the towering peaks of the mountain range slowly fading into the background. The landscape transforms, from sharp rocky slopes to gently rolling hills and flat stretches of land. Winter has laid claim over everything, casting the countryside in an ethereal white shroud.

At night, we set up a makeshift camp in the heart of a dense grove. The stars twinkle down at us from a clear, ink-black sky, providing the only light in the pervasive darkness. We huddle together for warmth, Thunder and Rain acting as living heaters for Silence and the pups. The bitter chill seeps into our bones, but we're safe, at least for the night.

The drone sits silent and cold in my pack. Its sudden activation a few days ago sent a ripple of fear through us, a reminder that our past is always just a step behind, waiting to catch up. But now, away from the mountain, away from the echo of engines, we can afford to breathe, if only for a little while.

FEBRUARY 18, YEAR UNKNOWN

As we move farther away from danger, my mind begins to turn back towards the vials safely tucked away in my sling. Each tiny glass tube represents a mystery - a mystery that could hold the key to saving countless lives, and perhaps, changing the course of this doomed world.

Without the facilities, equipment, and manpower of a functional lab, testing and understanding these vials will be a daunting task. But there's something I can do. As a former soldier, I've got a solid scientific background and a rudimentary understanding of the virus that's decimated the world. I've been living with this virus inside me, coexisting with it in a strange symbiosis that I barely understand.

I have to draw upon my past knowledge, my instincts, and my experiences in this new world. I decide to start with the most direct method of all - testing my own blood. If my blood holds the key to my survival, as well as the antidote to the virus, then it could provide answers.

In the cabin, I find an old first aid kit. It's pretty rudimentary, but it contains a syringe. The idea of drawing my own blood isn't exactly pleasant, but it's a step I need to take. Silence, who's been watching quietly, steps in to help.

Once we have a small sample, I study it as best I can under the dim cabin light. The black color, the thick viscosity, the way it reacts when I introduce a tiny amount of pure blood to it... Every little change, every response, could hold a clue. And perhaps, when I figure it out, we can test the contents of the vials, comparing them with my blood.

This could be a long, tiring process with a lot of trial and error. But right now, it's our only chance. And more than anything, it's a chance to fight back, to reclaim our lives without any military strings attached.

FEBRUARY 19, YEAR UNKNOWN

Today I sought Silence's help in the experiment. I needed a sample of uninfected, human blood for comparison. I explained to her the procedure and she initially seemed receptive, but as I prepared the needle, her demeanor changed abruptly.

Her face drained of color and she backed away from me, panic flickering in her eyes. "No," she mouthed, wrapping her arms protectively around her belly.

I was taken aback by her reaction. It was unlike her to show fear, especially to such a simple request. I tried to reassure her, tell her it would be quick, almost painless, but she refused to listen.

It was like a wall had been erected between us. Silence is usually so calm and collected, but now she seemed almost... scared. And that scared me. What could have possibly triggered such a reaction? What was she hiding?

Her refusal has presented me with a new challenge in my quest to understand the virus and these vials, but more than that, it has brought up a new mystery, one that could shake the foundations of the trust we've built.

I know Silence is a survivor, just like me. But today, I realized there might be much more to her story that I don't know, things she's been carrying with her, secret and buried. And I can't help but wonder... what else doesn't she want me to see? She sits now with her back to me, moaning lullabies to her baby. My thoughts are unclear. Hard to think about the way forward with this new conflict upon us.

FEBRUARY 20, YEAR UNKNOWN

Today was quiet, mostly. I felt a need for solitude, a need to breathe in the crisp winter air and clear my mind of the doubts that had cropped up. I took Thunder and ventured away from our temporary home, scouting the surroundings and keeping my senses alert for any signs of danger.

Silence and Rain stayed behind, a formidable pair looking after the younglings. As Thunder and I moved silently through the barren trees, I marveled at the peace the forest offered. The world was cruel, but in moments like this, it almost felt... serene.

But as night crept in, the silence was broken by a lone howl echoing through the hills, a chilling reminder of the world we were living in. I recognized it as the call of a wolf, probably in search of a meal or calling out to its pack.

Thunder grew tense underneath me, and I patted his side to calm him. I decided to head back, not wanting to risk an encounter with a pack of hungry wolves. My mind raced with thoughts of potential threats, the wolf's howl a stark reminder of the peril that lingered just beyond our tranquil hideaway.

Every night brings with it a new dread, a new challenge. But together, we've managed to brave the darkest storms. Tonight will be no different. I just hope the morning brings with it brighter prospects.

FEBRUARY 21, YEAR UNKNOWN

Today brought a glimmer of hope. As we wandered deeper into the wilderness, we stumbled upon an unexpected gem—a solid, sturdy building seemingly untouched by the decay of the world around it. It was an old ranger station, set in the heart of the forest.

From the outside, it seemed unassuming, half-hidden by tall

pines, its roof blanketed with a thick layer of snow. But as we approached it, I felt a surge of hope. Its stone walls were intact, its windows secure, and the door was reinforced with heavy iron. It felt secure, safe, and for the first time in a while, it felt like home.

With minimal effort, we cleared out the cobwebs and the dust that had settled over the years. The interior was simple, but it was dry and warm, a welcoming contrast to the cold winter outside.

We managed to fortify the entrances, setting traps and barriers outside. Silence, ever so resourceful, found a collection of dried herbs in a locked cabinet, a priceless find in our current world. Thunder, meanwhile, seemed to approve of our new abode, finding a cozy corner to nestle in.

As I write this, the wind howls outside, but its icy bite can't reach us here. For the first time in a long time, I find myself looking forward to tomorrow. Our new stronghold, this small island of safety amidst the chaos, feels like a new beginning, a new chapter in our journey to survive.

FEBRUARY 22, YEAR UNKNOWN

After securing the stronghold, I took some time to tinker with the remnants of the military drone. Its circuits and wirings, so delicately entwined, held an eerie semblance of life within them. There was something unsettling about the technology, how its purpose had been twisted in this broken world. Yet, it held answers, I was sure of it.

As I worked, my thoughts drifted to the vials. Their weight seemed to grow heavier each day, a constant reminder of the deadly chase I was embroiled in. The military's lust for them...it gnawed at me. But why?

Was it a cure as they had claimed? The idea twisted and turned in my mind, but it didn't fit. These were men who showed no remorse in gunning down a child. Who discarded me like an empty shell when they thought I had outlived my use. To them, the end justified the means, no matter the cost.

Yet, they risked so much for these vials. Why? Could it be a weapon? A new strain of the virus, perhaps? A tool to eradicate the undead? Or maybe to control them? These possibilities floated around in my mind, but nothing seemed to fit snugly. The pieces were there, but the puzzle remained unsolved.

For now, I kept the vials close, their secrets still locked within. But one thing was certain - whatever they contained, it was potent enough to drive men to extremes. I needed to figure it out, before they found us again.

FEBRUARY 23, YEAR UNKNOWN

Rain joins me as I continue to work with the drone. I've missed her company. Life's been hard, and I've found myself so caught up in our survival that I've neglected to spend time with her. Her gentle nature haunts her eyes.

As she nudges her nose into my hand, I'm reminded of Silence. Her quiet strength, her calm demeanor... Suddenly, the drone shifts innocently in my clumsy hand, catching the afternoon sun and sending a spear of light directly into my eyes. My head throbs instantly, an all too familiar pain shooting through my skull.

My vision blurs, replaced by another scene - a memory? I'm back in the sterile white of a military lab, a soldier again. The prick of a needle in my arm. A burning sensation as something is injected into my veins.

Beside me, another soldier - is that me? - undergoes the same procedure. But something's not right. The medics rush about, panic in their eyes. They're strapping him down, but he's struggling, fighting.

Then, all hell breaks loose. The straps snap as he transforms, not into a zombie, but something else - a monstrous creature, its size and strength beyond anything human. Its howls echo through the lab, and amidst the screams and chaos, I feel a deep sense of dread.

Suddenly, I'm back in the present, Rain's worried eyes staring into mine. The memory fades, leaving behind a cold fear. Was that my past? Or was it a warning of what's to come? I have to find out.

FEBRUARY 24, YEAR UNKNOWN

Spent the day recuperating from the seizure. The pain lingers, throbbing at my temples, but I've managed to push it to the back of my mind. I can't afford to be incapacitated, not with so much at stake.

Rain sat with me most of the day, her warm presence a comforting balm to the chaos of my thoughts. Her kindness reminds me of Silence, and I find myself questioning how they ended up with me, in this world of horror and uncertainty.

Spent the night sifting through the fragments of my past that have started to resurface. The memories are disjointed, like shattered glass. The beast, that monstrous creature, haunts my thoughts. I can't escape the feeling that it's crucial to our situation, to Silence's secret, to the mystery of the vials.

FEBRUARY 25, YEAR UNKNOWN

Silence is on edge today, her eyes distant, her movements sharp. The secret she carries is a weight on her shoulders. She won't look at me, avoids my gaze whenever I try to engage her in conversation.

Spent the day continuing my work on the drone. The incessant beeping seems to have stopped, but I worry it has already given away our location.

The children are growing so quickly, their development unnaturally accelerated. Rain watches them with a mixture of pride and confusion. I share her sentiments. We are living in strange times.

FEBRUARY 26, YEAR UNKNOWN

I've been remembering more and more about my past. Visions of labs, injections, soldiers and that beast...it's all linked, I'm sure of it.

I've decided to confront Silence about my suspicions. She holds answers, I know she does. I need to know the truth if we are to survive. Tomorrow, I will ask her.

FEBRUARY 27, YEAR UNKNOWN

In the quiet of the morning, Silence approaches me before I can make the first move. Her steps are hesitant, her features drawn in a mask of worry. She mimes to me, words she can't or won't say, her gestures sharp and deliberate. I watch as she points towards me and Thunder, shaking her head vigorously. Then she points at Rain, nodding.

I interpret her message as best as I can - she was cured like Rain, not a zombie like Thunder and I? But her frustration flares when I speak this out loud, and she brings her fist down hard on the steel table. The table buckles and concertinas like a toy under her unnatural strength.

She looks horrified at her own display, fear and regret etched on her face. Then, she's running, her footsteps echoing in the large, empty room. I let her go, left in the dust of her departure, still trying to piece together the puzzle she's left behind. It's clear now that she holds more secrets than I could have imagined, and the implications are as heavy as they are alarming.

FEBRUARY 28, YEAR UNKNOWN

I never expected to see what I saw tonight. The evening started peacefully, even happily. I had spent some time crafting a small twig doll, a token of peace, I suppose, for Silence. She had been upset earlier in the day, a reaction to her newfound strength perhaps. We'd had a small breakthrough, a brief moment of connection when I handed her the doll. A smile, a touch of my arm, it was something to hold onto. I went outside for air, and that's when the calm shattered.

Without any warning, the military men were there, surrounding me. Their ambush was swift and brutal. I only managed to decapitate one of them before they overpowered me with an electrical cattle gun, leaving me helpless on the ground while they barged into our sanctuary. I smelled the sickening aroma of vanilla before I even saw their leader's face. They were looking for something. It didn't take them long. Vanilla held up the vials in his hand like a treasure found, a look of satisfaction on his face that made my blood run cold.

The scene that followed was an unimaginable chaos. Thunder and Rain sprang into action, their instincts and fierce loyalty driving them to protect us all. Thunder bit into a soldier's face, wrenching him to the ground screaming while Rain lunged at another. She found flesh, but they were outnumbered and outgunned, and a deafening crack in the air stopped the attack.

Then came the moment that will forever be etched in my memory. Vanilla, his upper lip glistening (in anticipation?) picked up Silence's baby by the scruff of her neck, lifting her high and letting the wail of distress echo in the room. I could only see the scene reflected in the moonlit window - a grotesque mirror image that I couldn't escape from. There was a perverse glee in his eyes. I'd seen it before as he watched me in their compound. Had seen it again when he shot the zombie child.

Silence... she changed. Her body contorted and shifted, morphing into a powerful, terrifying form. A wolf on hind legs, with fierce eyes and muscles rippling beneath her fur. She moved with a speed and strength I'd never seen, tearing through the soldiers with ferocity and rage. The commander who held the baby aloft was frozen in terror as Silence transformed before him. He lost control of his bladder, a wet stain spreading across the front of his uniform. She held his gaze, a growl resonating deep within her as she savored the impending retribution. She lunged, her jaws clamping around his neck in a swift, lethal bite. His scream was cut off abruptly, and his head torn unceremoniously from his shoulders, a grim reminder of the price of their intrusion.

She cradled her child away from the headless leader's dead hands as his body fell down, and she disappeared into the night, letting him crumple loudly to the floor. His morbid finale.

We burned it all down. Left them in there and erased all traces of them.
Now, I'm here, sitting in the ruins of our sanctuary, the lingering scent of burnt wood filling my nostrils. Thunder and Rain are nearby, their bodies still tense from the fight. And Silence... I don't know what to make of her. What I witnessed tonight was not just a woman fighting to protect her child, but a beast unleashed.

This place, this sanctuary we had built, is now a monument to a terrifying revelation. Our family has been ripped apart once again, by the same people who had ripped me from them once before. We've lost Silence, a friend, a companion, and a confounding mystery. And yet, despite everything, there's a part of me that is terrified not of what Silence has become, but what she might do next.

FEBRUARY 29, YEAR UNKNOWN

Thunder and I left at first light, the pain in my head making the morning light even more piercing. The air was still bitter cold, the kind of cold that seems to seep into your very bones. We made our way along the track Silence and the baby had taken, fear gnawing at my gut as I thought of Silence, naked and defenseless in this frozen wilderness, with a newborn baby to care for.

We followed the trail, tracking her scent and the distinctive prints left by the enormous wolf creature she had transformed into. The tracks led us to the edge of a creek, where we found them huddled together. Silence, her skin almost blue from the cold, was lying on the ground, her body curled protectively around her tiny, whimpering child.

Silence had changed back to her human form, her body shivering uncontrollably. Her eyes were bloodshot, a dark red from the trauma, and her face was swollen beyond recognition. Hideous bruising from the transformation. She looked up as we approached, her eyes wide with fear and determination. Her teeth chattered as she reached out a trembling hand towards me, clutching at the air.

Thunder whinnied, nudging my arm. I dropped to my knees beside her, wrapping my coat around her frail body. We had to get her and the baby out of this cold, and fast.

MARCH 1, YEAR UNKNOWN

Today has been quiet, a stark contrast to the violent events of the past few nights. We have been huddled by the fire, Silence lying under a heap of blankets, cradling her baby. I have done my best to take on a fatherly role, trying to keep the baby entertained so Silence can get some much-needed rest.

Her little girl, we have named her Harmony, is a bundle of curiosity. She has Silence's eyes, bright and attentive, always watching, always learning. She's already trying to move around on her own, crawling across the rug in front of the fireplace, an impressive feat considering her age.

In these moments, the simplicity of taking care of a child, the world outside seems almost distant, the horrors we face daily seem less tangible. It's a small silver lining in this chaotic existence, and I find solace in these moments.

As I watch Silence sleep, her face peaceful, Harmony nuzzled into her chest, I can't help but feel a warmth spreading in my chest. This is my family now, unconventional as it may be. We are all survivors, all broken in our own ways, yet together we manage to find a sense of normalcy.

Today has been a good day, a calming of the storm. And for now, that's enough.

MARCH 2, YEAR UNKNOWN

It was just after dawn when Silence woke up. I'd been keeping vigil, stoking the fire to keep the cabin warm. I'd been too afraid to sleep, too afraid that I'd wake up to find her gone. So when I heard a soft groan, I rushed over to her side.

Her eyes fluttered open, revealing those piercing blue orbs that always seemed to see right through me. For a moment, she seemed disoriented, her gaze flickering from me to the fire and back again. And then, realization dawned on her, and her eyes filled with a palpable sense of relief.

"Alive," she mouthed. Her voice was hoarse, unused, but it was the most beautiful sound I'd ever heard.

"Yes," I replied, tears pricking my eyes. "You are."
Silence was an enigma wrapped in a riddle. She was both fiercely protective and incredibly gentle, a stark contradiction that never failed to astound me. Even in her terrifying canine form, there had been a softness in her eyes, a plea for understanding that tugged at my heartstrings. Her strength was beyond anything I'd ever seen, but it was her capacity for love, especially for her daughter, Harmony, that left the lasting impression on me. The way she fought against her curse, trying to retain her humanity, was a lesson I would never forget.

Throughout the day, she remained quiet, absorbing the events that had transpired. I told her about the soldiers, about her transformation and her instinctual protection of Harmony. She listened silently, her expression unreadable. But when I told her that we had escaped, that we were safe, I saw a flicker of relief pass over her features.

She spent the rest of the day regaining her strength. I watched as she held Harmony close, the bond between mother and child so strong it was almost tangible. I saw a future for us, a hope I hadn't dared to imagine before.

Today, we've taken a step closer to that future. Silence is recovering, and with every passing moment, we grow stronger. We're going to get through this, together. We have to.

MARCH 3, YEAR UNKNOWN

Silence woke up today looking stronger than she has in days. She sat up, cradling Harmony in her arms, and a small smile curved her lips. It was a sight that warmed me to my core. Silence has a strength that is undeniably awe-inspiring. Even after everything she's been through, she rises, she endures.

And it seems Harmony is taking after her mother. The tiny bundle of joy is growing stronger each day. She wriggles constantly in her mother's arms, eager to explore the world around her. She's already started teething, which is surprising considering her age. But then again, she is Silence's daughter. And if there's anything I've learned about this family, it's that they are anything but ordinary.

In a way, watching Harmony grow so quickly is bittersweet. In another world, under different circumstances, we would have had the luxury to watch her grow slowly, to savor each new milestone. But this is our reality, and we adapt. We find joy in the small things and hold onto them, cherishing each moment because we don't know what tomorrow will bring.

But for now, we are here, we are safe, and we are together. And that's all that matters.

MARCH 4, YEAR UNKNOWN

There's an unease in the air, a tension that follows us around as we figure out our next steps. We're not the most conventional family, and our current predicament is something out of a fantasy novel. Two zombie men, a zombie horse, a werewolf, a faithful dog, and Harmony - a little bundle of strength and joy that fills our days with warmth.

We're quite the motley crew, and our strengths are as unique as our forms. We each bring something to the table, and as I look at our little group, I can't help but feel a surge of hope. We're more than just survivors; we're a force to be reckoned with.

The issue that has been on my mind, however, is Whisky. The man is now a shadow of his former self, a gnarled zombie with an insatiable hunger. His presence near the pups and Harmony sends a shiver down my spine. He was once a trusted companion, but now, I can't help but feel a sense of danger. He needs to be kept at a distance, at least until we can figure out a way to ensure the safety of the little ones. Whisky was...complicated. Even though he was a man turned zombie, there was a certain innocence about him. His transformation hadn't stripped him of his humanity entirely. Rather, it seemed to have amplified his most basic instincts and emotions. He could be fierce and protective one moment, docile and affectionate the next. Despite the challenges he faced, Whisky held on to his spirit, refusing to succumb to the monstrosity of his new form. His struggle was a mirror to my own, a constant reminder of the cost of survival in our broken world.

The vials remain a mystery. Their contents have the potential to either save or destroy us, and the uncertainty is unsettling. The military is undoubtedly after them, and we need to be ready for when they come.

The drone is our wild card, a device that could potentially turn the tide of the impending battle in our favor. If only I could figure out how to operate it to its full potential.

Despite the challenges, there's an underlying determination in all of us. We've been pushed to the brink, and it's time to push back. We've lost too much, sacrificed too much to back down now. Our resolve is stronger than ever. This fight is about more than survival; it's about reclaiming our freedom, our right to exist without fear. It's time to make our stand.

MARCH 7, YEAR UNKNOWN

The moon is our only guide as we journey through the night. Silence, with Harmony nestled against her chest in a papoose, leads the way. Whisky rides atop Thunder, the horse seemingly undisturbed by the zombie man on his back. The pups snuggle against my chest, their tiny bodies warm inside their own papoose. Rain and I run in tandem, our footfalls softened by the blanket of grass beneath us.

We are heading toward the heart of danger, the military base where our foes are likely preparing for our eventual showdown. But we aren't planning to walk straight into their fortress. We need a distraction, something to draw their attention and forces away from their base, and we have just the place in mind: The Valley of the Dead.

Known among survivors for its dangerous terrain and high concentration of zombies, the valley would make for a perfect diversion. If we can rouse the zombies and steer them toward the military base, we'll create the perfect chaos for us to sneak in unnoticed.

The stakes are high. Every step we take is a calculated risk. But we have no choice. It's time to fight back, to reclaim our lives from the hands of those who have wronged us. We have a plan, and we have each other. In the end, that's all we really need.

But first, we have a valley to cross.

MARCH 8th

We crossed the frozen lake once more, the memory of our last visit hanging over us like an icy specter. As we moved carefully over the slick surface, the behemoth rose again from beneath the ice, sending me sprawling to the ground. The titan of a zombie towered over us, an echo of the terror he used to sow.

But it was Silence who saved the day.

With the eerie control that had once shaken us to our cores, she shifted halfway to her other form. Her eyes, instantly bloodshot gave the illusion of a glowing red intensity and one arm almost rippled with the muscular form of the wolf. The powerful limb shot forward, seizing the massive zombie by the throat and pinning him against a tree, his feet kicking uselessly in the air.

We watched in stunned silence as the gentle woman, now a commanding force of nature, dominated the scene. But the biggest shock came when she spoke. Her voice was hoarse from disuse, a single word filled with command: "Vial."

In her grasp, the giant zombie was docile, his thrashing stilled. Following her instructions, I approached warily and administered a single drop of the red vial into the zombie's eye. The transformation was instant. His grotesque form slackened, and he turned into a regular man, albeit a huge one. Tears started streaming down his face, a stark display of human emotion we hadn't seen in the infected.

"The other," Silence ordered. Hesitation flashed through me, but I handed her the blue vial, recalling our previous encounter with it. She forced a drop into the man's mouth. What happened next was beyond belief. The man's body swelled and transformed into a form similar to Silence's wolf state, the transformation retaining his docility.

In the space of moments, we had witnessed two miracles: the return of the humanity of a zombie and the birth of another creature of strength. Silence had given us a beacon of hope - and perhaps a new ally in our fight against the military.

MARCH 9, YEAR UNKNOWN

After witnessing the dual transformation of the giant, a plan began to form in our minds. We were no longer a small group of survivors, outnumbered and outgunned. We had two powerful, controlled werewolves and a functioning drone at our disposal.

We spent the day in animated discussion, our spirits buoyed by the previous day's discoveries. The drone, previously a source of anxiety and fear, was now looked upon as an asset. Its aerial advantage could provide a necessary distraction for the military, drawing their attention and resources.

Silence was the one who suggested it, her voice still raspy but growing stronger each time she used it. We could use the drone as a decoy. Rig it to broadcast its signal, tricking the military into thinking we were elsewhere. Meanwhile, we could approach the military base from another direction, relatively unobserved.

We agreed unanimously. It was a simple but effective plan. It gave us hope. For the first time in a long while, I felt like we had the upper hand. We spent the rest of the day preparing for our mission, each of us filled with a sense of purpose and resolve.

Our new allies had tilted the odds in our favor. We were no longer running scared. Now, we were taking the fight to them.

MARCH 10, YEAR UNKNOWN

Today was a test of our courage and resolve. As we began our dangerous trek back towards the military base, the world seemed to press against us with all its post-apocalyptic weight. We walked through barren landscapes, once teeming with life, now filled with haunting echoes of a world that was no more.

As we ventured further into the heartland, we began to encounter zombies. Single walkers at first, easy to avoid, but then we saw larger hordes in the distance. Even though we had the means to subdue them, we decided it was best to conserve our vial supply and avoid unnecessary conflicts. Thanks to Silence's sharp senses and quick thinking, we successfully navigated around these hordes, leaving them none the wiser of our presence.

The wolves proved to be more challenging. Their packs roamed the forests, their eerie howls piercing the silence of the night. Their eyes shone like tiny stars in the darkness, a chilling sight that sent shivers down my spine. But, again, Silence proved invaluable. Her transformation had given her a connection with these creatures. More than once, she stared them down, asserting her dominance. It was remarkable to witness, her standing tall, eyes ablaze, a primal force that the wolves respected.

We continued our journey, each step bringing us closer to our ultimate goal. The hardship of today, I am convinced, is necessary. It is tempering us, preparing us for the fight to come. Our spirits remain unbroken. Our resolve, unwavering. Tomorrow, we march on.

MARCH 11, YEAR UNKNOWN

The low hum of military aircraft echoed across the expanse today, an unwelcome and haunting sound. We had to be more careful now, any small mistake could give away our position. So, we decided to use the abundant snow as our camouflage. We dug out small snow caves, just big enough for each of us to fit in. Whisky, with his immense size, offered to dig for us, a task he performed with an uncanny calmness that belied his fearsome appearance.

Silence cradled Harmony in her arms as they lay hidden beneath the snow. The baby, sensing her mother's tension, remained unusually quiet, her innocent eyes wide with curiosity. As for the pups, they seemed to enjoy this new game of 'hide and seek', their tails wagging in excitement. We wrapped them in extra layers of clothing to protect them from the cold, their small bodies snuggled against mine, their heat a welcome comfort in the chilly surroundings.

As for Rain, we had a different plan. She was to remain away from our hiding spots with Thunder. Their task was to lead the military away in case we were spotted. Rain, being an excellent tracker, was more than capable of leading them on a wild goose chase while keeping herself and Thunder safe. Their presence not far from us was comforting, a reassurance that we had a plan in place.

As night fell, the noise of the aircraft faded away, replaced by the soft hush of falling snow. We slowly emerged from our hideouts, dusting off the snow, and checked on each other. Harmony was sleeping soundly, unfazed by the day's events, the pups were playfully bounding around, their energy seemingly endless. Our spirits lifted at these sights, reminding us of what we were fighting for.

Tomorrow, we continue our journey, our mission clearer than ever.

MARCH 12, YEAR UNKNOWN

Today was a mixed bag of emotions. As dawn broke, our behemoth werewolf companion, who'd been a silent and formidable ally thus far, began to revert back to his original state - a frightened, babbling man, teetering on the edge of sanity. His hulking body shrank, and his once fearsome demeanor gave way to confusion and fear. He stumbled around aimlessly, clutching his head as if trying to keep his thoughts in place. It was a pitiful sight, but it brought forth a harsh reality.

The power of the blue vial was temporary.

A difficult decision had to be made. We didn't know how many times we could use the vial before running out, or whether the man's body could even handle repeated transformations. The humane choice, albeit the riskier one, was to keep him in his human form until it was absolutely necessary for him to transform. With every passing second, the stakes of our mission became more apparent.

Silence held Harmony close, her eyes hardened with determination. Rain stood by, vigilant and alert, her protective instincts in overdrive. Whisky was surprisingly calm, his zombie-like state offering an eerie sense of tranquility. As for the pups, they were blissfully unaware of the dangers lurking around us, their innocence a welcome distraction amidst the brewing storm.

We move forward, knowing the road is fraught with peril, but the light at the end of the tunnel is clearer than ever.

MARCH 13, YEAR UNKNOWN

The sun hadn't fully crested the horizon when the first signs of tension flared. Whisky, perhaps sensing weakness or maybe it was the zombie part of him simply responding to his nature, lunged at the newly human man. I don't know if Whisky was being territorial, or if the sight of a weakened human triggered his predatory instincts. Regardless, it was clear I had to intervene before things escalated.

With Harmony and the pups asleep and Silence too protective of her child to risk moving, it fell on me to maintain the peace.

I moved quickly, throwing myself in between Whisky and the terrified man, pulling Whisky away. The force of my grip made him yelp in surprise. He snapped around, teeth bared, and for a moment I thought he would turn on me.

I held his gaze, my stance unyielding, asserting my dominance in our little pack. He held my gaze for a moment longer before breaking eye contact and backing away, head lowered. I gave him a stern pat, a silent reprimand but also a reassurance of sorts - I wasn't against him, but I needed him to respect the boundaries I had set.

The man was shaking, his eyes wide with fear as he stared at me. I offered him a reassuring smile, and for the first time since we started this journey, he smiled back.

Despite the tension, the incident served as a reminder of the power dynamics within our group, and of the delicate balance we needed to maintain. The danger within could be just as treacherous as the dangers without. This journey demanded not just physical strength but also psychological resilience.

Our motley crew seemed to understand this. Once the excitement was over, everyone settled down quickly. We were back on the move soon, under the watchful eye of a rosy dawn.

Despite the initial hiccup, the day was productive. We covered a good distance without any other incident, but we are still far from the military base. The sense of unease grows with each passing day, but we press on, each step taking us closer to our goal.

The knowledge that the vials in my sling could either be our salvation or our ruin weighs heavy on my mind. But I know that to get through this, we need to stick together, protect each other, and remember that we are stronger as a group than as individuals.

We carry on, towards the unknown, steeling ourselves for what lies ahead.

MARCH 14, YEAR UNKNOWN

Our journey today brought us to a sight that made my blood run cold and anger flare up like a wildfire. A ramshackle camp of survivors had been set up in a clearing, but this was no place of refuge. It was a stronghold, fortified by walls of impaled zombie heads on wooden stakes, their rotting faces contorted in eternal screams.

The smell was unbearable, a sickening mixture of decay, fear, and burnt flesh that permeated the air. But what truly turned my stomach was the sound that carried over the disgusting tableau — the sounds of coarse laughter and drunken shouting, echoing through the cold evening air.

I saw them then — human soldiers, ragged but armed, around a fire. And behind them, penned like animals, were others. Women and children, all zombies, looking terrified and hopeless. The sight was gut-wrenching. My heart pounded in my chest as I surveyed the camp, each beat a call to action.

It was Silence who pulled me back into reality. Her hand on my arm, her grip tight. She was staring at me, her eyes wide, fearful. For a moment, I was confused. And then I realized, it was not fear for herself or Harmony. It was fear for me. She was warning me not to rush in, not to let my anger control me.

I had a choice to make. The easy one would have been to turn around, to protect Silence, Harmony, and our pups. But then I thought of the captives, the innocents suffering at the hands of those who should be their allies, their fellow survivors. How could we call ourselves human if we ignored such cruelty?

My mind raced. I needed a plan, a strategy that would free the captives without endangering my family. I felt a cold determination settle over me as I looked back at the camp. I made my decision then. I would not let these atrocities continue.

I couldn't help but feel a little thankful for the military training I'd had in my previous life. It's strange how things you thought you'd left behind come back to you when you need them the most.

We retreated into the woods to plan our attack. We had the cover of darkness, our own surprising abilities, and most importantly, the element of surprise. Tonight, we were not just survivors; we were warriors.

The night is going to be long and dangerous, and the moon, peeking out from behind the clouds, will be the only witness to our battle. But I swear on whatever is left of the civilized world, we will not let those monsters continue their reign of terror.

Tonight, we fight.

MARCH 15, YEAR UNKNOWN

Today started with hope and determination but ended in despair. We fell right into their trap. The captives were just bait, luring us into a false sense of purpose and distracting us from the real danger.

As we planned our attack, the ground beneath me gave way. It was a pit trap, and I fell hard, tumbling into darkness. The next thing I knew, I was trapped, a thick metal grate separating me from my family. The look of horror and disbelief on Silence's face as I fell will forever be etched in my memory.

I scrambled to my feet, shouting at them to run. But it was too late. The forest around us erupted in a cacophony of shouts, gunshots, and the terrifying sound of mechanical equipment. The undergrowth swarmed with soldiers, swathed in night-vision goggles and armed to the teeth. Before we could react, we were surrounded.

A sharp, painful shock was delivered by a cattle prod, forcing me to the ground. I looked up in time to see Silence and the pups being roughly restrained. Whisky, displaying an amazing sense of loyalty, fought back fiercely. But he was outnumbered and, like the rest of us, was soon overpowered.

A figure separated from the chaos and walked towards the pit. It was the sly, wicked-eyed leader we had encountered before. His smug, triumphant grin made my blood boil. The vials were displayed prominently in his hand, catching the faint moonlight. I realized with a sinking feeling that our mission was over before it even began.

"I was wondering if you'd even heed my invitation," he gloated, his voice echoing off the cold metal. He turned towards his soldiers, instructing them to transport us to the military facility. "Secure the specimens," he commanded.

We were not even their enemies anymore; we were their experiments. My heart pounded with fear and rage as I saw Silence and Harmony, so terrified and helpless. But my own helplessness was far greater.

As the soldiers began to move us, I looked up at the night sky, pleading with any power that might still exist in this godforsaken world. We were heading straight into the lion's den. We were prisoners. The fight had only just begun.

MARCH 16, YEAR UNKNOWN

We have become prisoners, like the very people we sought to save. The irony isn't lost on me. Trapped inside this cold, steel box on wheels, I can't help but wonder how our noble mission had turned into this. I've watched as they loaded Silence, Harmony, the pups, Rain, Whisky, and even Thunder, onto a separate truck. Their faces, filled with terror and confusion, are a sight I'll never forget.

The trucks are like cages on wheels. They took no chances, sedating even our animal companions. I could see the tranq darts sticking out from their sides. The sight of Whisky and Thunder, two creatures of such immense strength and resilience, reduced to this state was heartbreaking.

I, on the other hand, was left conscious. A small victory, perhaps, or a cruel punishment. Locked inside my solitary truck cell, I can only watch the world whizzing past through the small slits that serve as windows. The military trucks form a formidable convoy, each manned by multiple soldiers, their weapons ready and alert. We are headed straight into the heart of their operation.

The journey is long, the road rough and winding. Every bump, every turn only heightens my sense of dread. I catch glimpses of the outside world, a world we had been surviving in, fighting for. The forests, the mountains, even the desolate wastelands. It all seems so peaceful from this vantage point. A stark contrast to the chaos we are about to walk into.

I can't help but wonder what awaits us. Is it death? Or something even worse? All I know is that we need to survive, to fight. If not for us, then for Harmony, for the pups. For a chance at a better future. For now, all I can do is watch and wait. But when the time comes, I'll be ready.

MARCH 17th

Under the cover of a moonless night, we are led into the heart of the enemy's den. The military compound looms ominously against the starless sky, a monstrous silhouette devoid of any welcoming warmth. Even the wind seems to wail in mournful howls as we inch closer, its chilling gusts seeping through the slits in the truck, teasing my skin with its icy touch.

The distant howls echo ominously through the night, their eerie cries an unnerving soundtrack to our grim procession. I strain to identify the source, but the echoes seem to warp and distort the sounds until they are barely recognizable. Are they the wails of zombies or the cries of wolves? Or perhaps, they are the cries of both, a twisted symphony of the lost and damned. The thought sends a shiver down my spine.

As we enter the compound, I am gripped by a sense of dread, a feeling I have not felt since...the outbreak. I remember the chaos, the fear, the desperation. The faces of my colleagues as we scrambled to save what we could, the despairing screams of those we couldn't. My mind strains against the torrent of memories, each more gruesome than the last, threatening to drown me in their depths. I can feel the beast within stirring, its fury mirroring my own, a wild and untamed force pushing against the frayed edges of my control.

Yet, amid the tempest of emotions, I force myself to observe, to remember. Every detail, every nuance could be crucial. The layout of the compound, the positions of the guards, the codes on the doors, anything and everything could be a potential lifeline. But my mind is a haze of red, clouded by anger and fear, the details blurring into an indistinguishable mass. I curse under my breath, frustration gnawing at my calm facade.

But for now, I can do little but wait, and bide my time. For when the time comes, the beast and I will be ready. As a great writer by the name of Dylan once said, "We will not go gently into that good night. We will rage, rage against the dying of the light."

MARCH 18, YEAR UNKNOWN

As the cold night descends, they separate us. They strip us of our possessions, our weapons, and our companions. I am left alone in a dank, cold cell with nothing but my thoughts for company. The cold seeps into my bones, numbing my senses and slowly freezing my resolve.

MARCH 19, YEAR UNKNOWN

From the cell next to mine, I can hear the pitiful sobbing of the human wolf. His cries echo off the cold stone walls, reverberating through the haunting silence like a ghostly melody. I close my eyes, wishing there was something I could do to help, to ease his suffering. But I am as helpless as he is, a prisoner of circumstances beyond my control.

MARCH 20, YEAR UNKNOWN

The silence of the compound is eerie, unsettling. The absence of sound is so profound that it feels as if the world itself has stopped turning, as if time itself has stood still. There is no howling of wolves, no growling of zombies, no murmurs of hushed conversations. Only the solemn stillness of the night, the eerie quiet a stark contrast to the chaos that brought us here.

Once, in the dead of night, I hear the familiar whinny of Thunder. The sound brings a momentary respite, a fleeting connection to the world outside my cell. But as quickly as it comes, it is gone, swallowed by the oppressive silence.

"Partner up, Lance," Maddox's voice echoed through the night air as he emerged from the shadows on the other side of the bars. His silhouette was almost unrecognizable, twisted and grotesque as the moonlight bounced off his pale skin. He looked as if he needed medical attention.

Memories flooded back to me, of a time when Maddox and I worked side by side, part of an elite force trained to face humanity's worst fears. But that was before the world changed, before he changed.

"You and me," he continued, stepping into the light to reveal his horrifying visage, "We could rule this new world together."

A bitter taste filled my mouth as I remembered what he had done. His betrayal. His insane obsession with power. His twisted experiments... Silence. She was there. His assistant, another pawn in his game. Forced to endure such horrors for nothing but one man's power.

"Join you?" I spat, disgust welling up inside me, "After what you've done to the world? I'd rather die."

Maddox chuckled, his voice a guttural growl, "You don't get it, do you, Lance? We're the future. We are the evolution of humanity. The weak will die out, and the strong, us, we will rule."

There was a madness in his eyes, a delusion of grandeur. He truly believed he was the hero, the savior of humanity. But all I saw was a monster, a man who had let his ambition strip away his humanity.

"I won't ever join you, Maddox," I said, my voice steady, "You're no hero. You're a monster."

He snarled, his face a grimace of pain. But I didn't back down. I had made my choice, and I would fight till the end. Because unlike Maddox, I hadn't lost sight of what it meant to be human. He laughed loudly. A surreal moment. And then he was gone.

As the hours drag on, I cling to the hope that Rain, Silence, and the others are safe. I take small comfort in the knowledge that we are still alive, that we still have a fighting chance. We have survived the worst of the apocalypse, and we will survive this too. But as the darkness deepens, I can't shake off the gnawing fear that our trials are far from over.

MARCH 21, YEAR UNKNOWN

The silence is shattered in the dead of the night. The clamor outside my cell is deafening, a cacophony of panicked shouts, hurried footsteps, and the shrill ringing of alarms. The walls of my cell seem to shudder with the sudden onset of chaos. I rise to my feet, pressing my ear against the cold, damp wall in an attempt to make sense of the commotion.

"Code 5!" I hear someone shout, their voice strangled with fear. "Code 5!"

The heavy thud of boots against the stone floor grows louder as guards rush past my cell. I catch fragments of their hurried conversations, phrases like "breach in the west wall" and "containment failure." There are shouts for medical assistance and a flurry of orders being barked out, creating a confusing symphony of fear and disorder.

Despite the confusion, one thing becomes clear to me: something has gone horribly wrong. There has been a breach, a breakdown in their so-called security measures. I can't help but feel a surge of hope amidst the chaos. This could be our chance, our opportunity to escape. But, I am also filled with worry. The others... are they safe? What has happened?

With every fiber of my being, I long to break free from my confinement, to find my friends, to protect them. But for now, all I can do is wait, listen, and hope. In this madhouse of panic and fear, hope is all I have. It feels like the world is on fire, and I'm trapped in the inferno, waiting for the flames to reach me. But I'm not going down without a fight.

A silence descends upon the compound, a quiet so stark it feels unnatural, eerie. The electricity cuts off without warning, the hum of the generators dying away into nothing, and I realized as the darkness became total that I was alone again. The high-pitched whine of the electric lock on my cell fades and I push against the heavy door. With a groan of protest, it swings open.

Cautiously, I step into the dimly lit corridor, half-expecting to be jumped at any second. But nothing happens. No Maddox, No alarm. No guards. The maze of corridors stretch out before me, like the intestines of this hellish beast, and I traverse them with great care.

My heart nearly stops when I find Silence. She is strapped down to a table, her pale skin washed out in the eerie light. Tubes are hooked into her veins, connected to a machine that hums ominously. She's weak, her breaths coming out in small, ragged gasps. But she's alive.

I rush over to her, carefully pulling the tubes from her skin and undoing the restraints. Her eyes flutter open, cloudy with confusion and exhaustion. "Lance," she whispers hoarsely, her voice barely a whisper.

Suddenly, a chilling howl reverberates through the compound, followed by the unmistakable sound of gunfire and screams. The sound echoes around us, sending a shiver down my spine.

Something has gone terribly wrong.

Silence tries to stand, but her knees buckle. I catch her before she hits the floor, wrapping an arm around her waist to steady her. She clings to me, her fingers digging into my arm.

We have to get out of here.

A quick scan of the room reveals the torn and shredded clothes of Maddox, but no blood. He's transformed into something...and he's out there. But I also know he is not my main concern. We need to find the others, and we need to get out.

The fight is far from over. We move slowly through the compound, every creak and echo threatening to give away our position. The sight of Thunder brings a relieved sigh from my lips. Our loyal steed looks unharmed, albeit a little shaken up, and he quickly bounds to our side when he spots us. The dogs follow suit, their tails wagging furiously as they press themselves against our legs, whining in relief.

Our joy is short-lived though. The human man, the one who had been a wolf until just recently, refuses to come with us. He's huddled in a corner of his cell, his eyes wide with terror, shaking his head vigorously when we try to coax him out. Time is not on our side, so with a pang of regret, we leave him behind. He's made his choice.

The absence of Whisky hits us like a blow to the gut. He is nowhere to be found, and my heart clenches at the thought of leaving him behind. But we can't afford to search for him now. We need to escape this place.

As we move deeper into the compound, the distant sounds of chaos grow louder. Gunshots ring out sporadically, punctuated by screams and growls. The compound is in a state of panic and confusion, and we use this to our advantage. I can only hope that the others are safe, and that we can find them before it's too late.

In the cold, metallic corridors of the compound, fear hangs heavy in the air. But it's not just ours; it's a pervasive, tangible terror that seems to have taken hold of everyone in this godforsaken place.

Suddenly, the eerie silence is broken by the thudding of heavy boots against the steel grating. A group of soldiers bursts around the corner, stumbling over each other in their haste to escape from something. Their faces are pale and bloodied, their eyes wide and unseeing with stark, bone-deep fear.

They careen past us without a second glance, too consumed by their terror to pay us any mind. It's a chilling sight to behold. These men, who had so cruelly and casually torn us from our sanctuary, are now nothing more than frightened animals, running from an unseen predator.

And we are walking towards it. The thought is sobering. Whatever had these hardened soldiers in such a state of panic, we are heading directly into its path. Yet, we have no choice. We have to find Harmony. We press on, despite the gnawing fear in our guts, despite the screams and the clamor growing louder with each step. The unknown awaits us, but we will face it. For Harmony. For all of us.

We came upon a towering wall of concrete and steel, an impenetrable barrier that cut off our forward momentum. There was a heavy bunker door, locked and secured beyond our ability to force open. As we were weighing our options and considering a retreat, a disastrous twist of fate forced our hand.

An old, frayed electrical cable, discarded recklessly against the wall, sparked suddenly, igniting a bundle of dry insulation material. In moments, the corridor behind us was filled with thick, choking smoke and fiery tendrils that quickly consumed the narrow path.

We had no choice but to press forward into an engineer's tunnel, a small side passage that led deeper into the bowels of the compound. Thunder found it difficult to navigate the tight, winding passage, his large body barely squeezing through the confined space. The dogs and Silence had to crouch to fit through, with me leading the way. The smell of the burning corridor behind us fueled our urgency as we descended further into the unfamiliar, and the chilling echoes of terror above grew fainter with each step.

Despite the fear and uncertainty, there was a grim determination in our hearts. We had to find Harmony, and we would face whatever lay ahead. Whatever had been unleashed in the compound, it couldn't be worse than losing her. And so, we moved forward, deeper into the unknown.

We continued to traverse through the underbelly of the compound, navigating through dimly lit, long-abandoned tunnels. Their cold stone walls echoed with our soft footfalls, a whispering testament to our clandestine journey.

Our progress slowed as we found ourselves trapped in an old cavern, lost beneath the compound, its entrance obscured by fallen rubble and age-old debris. There was an unsettling silence that hung heavy in the air, punctuated only by the quiet drips of water from unseen sources.

There were no lights here, only the unsettling darkness, reaching out with its cold tendrils, ready to envelop us. The only glimmer of hope was a small shaft of light from a crevice high up in the cavern ceiling, too small for any of us to squeeze through, but enough to cast long, haunting shadows across our haggard faces.

As the cold seeped into our bones, we huddled together for warmth, the dogs lying protectively around us, their quiet panting the only sign of life in this subterranean crypt. There were no words spoken, only the unspoken promise of survival burning in our eyes. We were trapped, but we were together, united against the dark.

With no way forward, the day slipped into night, the distant hum of the compound far above the only reminder of the world we'd left behind. But even amidst the uncertainty, there was resolve. We had faced worse odds, and we would find a way out, for Harmony, for all of us.

As the new day dawned, we greeted it with renewed determination, for the tunnel may have been dark, but we carried the light within us. The journey continued...

Together, we attacked the solid wall of the tunnel, chipping away at the stubborn stone that barricaded our path. Silence, with her strength returning, was a force to be reckoned with, her fists striking the stone wall with a determination that reverberated throughout the tunnel.

Our efforts were rewarded when we discovered Whisky in a hidden part of the cavern. But our joy was cruelly snuffed out as a monstrous figure rose behind him, grotesque and terrifying. A beast larger than anything we had ever seen - a monstrous hybrid of wolf and zombie strength. Our military leader, his lust for power leading him to fuse himself with both species.

He towered over us, letting out a blood-curdling scream as he discarded Whisky's lifeless body with callous indifference. A pang of loss and despair gripped me, but I shoved it down, focusing instead on the small figure he held in his other arm. Harmony. Unharmed, but her wide eyes reflected the fear she must have felt. She was more than just an innocent child to him; she was a source of future serum, a commodity.

The sight of the monstrous man standing triumphant, Harmony clutched in his arm, ignited a fury within me that was more potent than any fear. The battle lines were drawn. It was time to end this.

Silence moved first, her maternal instincts overriding any sense of fear or self-preservation. With a guttural growl, she launched herself at the monster, her claws slashing through the air with deadly accuracy. She severed the beast's arm with one swift move, reclaiming Harmony in the same instant. The beast howled in pain, recoiling from the force of her attack. But its retaliation was swift and brutal, tearing a gaping wound into Silence's back and sending her crumpled form into a corner.

Thunder, reacting to the sight of his fallen companion, charged at the beast. But his attack was met with an effortless swipe, batting him away as if he weighed nothing. Rain growled menacingly, her pups yipping fiercely from behind her. Their small bodies were trembling, but their resolve was firm.

Meanwhile, I found myself desperately scrambling to put my plan into action. Tying a tight knot around my already wounded arm, I ignored the sharp sting of pain as I reopened the wound, allowing my blood to freely flow. The plan was simple - I needed the beast to ingest my blood. Yet, as I looked at the towering monster, a horrifying fusion of wolf and zombie, I knew it wouldn't be easy. But it was our only chance. We had to try.

Just as the situation was looking its bleakest, a thunderous sound echoed throughout the chamber. A hulking figure burst through the entrance, sending debris scattering in every direction. It was our gentle giant, but he was a wolf again, his form massive and imposing. Fearless and with a ferocity I had never seen before, he hurled himself directly at the monstrous beast.

The force of the impact was enormous, the two colossal beings colliding with a violence that shook the very foundations of the compound. They both crashed through the weakened wall, disappearing into the darkness of the cavern beyond. The room was left in a stunned silence, the lingering echoes of the collision slowly fading away.

As the echoes of the colossal clash dissipated, I turned to see Silence struggling to rise. Her body shuddered, rippling in its effort to heal. The wolfen energy within her was directed towards mending the gash in her back, pulling her away from her beastly form and back to her human self.

Gently, I offered her a hand, and she accepted with a nod of gratitude. I helped her to her feet and whispered words of encouragement to her. She cradled Harmony close to her chest, her love for her child unmistakable in her gaze. I pleaded with her to retreat, to take Rain and the pups and find a safer place in the compound. The worry in her eyes was clear, but she understood the necessity of the choice.

Assured of their safety, I turned back to the gaping hole in the wall. The sounds of the monstrous duel echoed from the cavern beyond, a cacophony of roars, howls, and the deafening crash of titanic bodies. Determination filled my heart as I moved forward, ready to face whatever lay ahead.

I entered the cavern just in time to see the monstrous military leader savagely wrench our giant werewolf companion apart. It was as if he were no more than a mere wishbone in the claws of the beast, the horrific crack reverberating throughout the chamber. The man-wolf's screams abruptly silenced, swallowed by the overwhelming darkness.

The beast turned, its monstrous gaze focusing solely on me. The twisted, grotesque features were barely recognizable as human anymore, a hideous amalgamation of human, wolf, and zombie. A wave of fury radiated off him, suffocating the air around us. His yellow eyes, filled with a savage rage, bore into me, acknowledging my presence.

This was it. The final face-off. The end game. I felt a rush of adrenaline coursing through my veins, my heart pounding with a raw determination. There was no turning back now. The time had come to end this nightmare once and for all.

As the night descended over us, an eerie calm settled over the compound. The harsh, fluorescent lights flickered sporadically in the darkness, casting long and ominous shadows. I could hear the hollow echo of my own footsteps, a lonely and unnerving sound that amplified the silence around me.

I could taste the imminent danger in the air, metallic and sharp. My heart pounded in my chest, a harsh drumbeat echoing my dread. The vials in my pocket felt cold and heavy against my skin, a constant reminder of the horrifying transformation that awaited me.

I could feel Maddox's presence, as tangible as the darkness that surrounded us. He was here, somewhere, lurking in the shadows, waiting. He was no longer the man I once knew. He had become something else entirely, something monstrous and inhuman.

Every instinct screamed at me to turn back, to find Silence and the others and escape. But I knew there was no turning back. I had to confront Maddox, for Silence, for our friends, and for the hope of a world that had been ravaged by his twisted ambitions.

Suddenly, the beating of helicopter blades filled the air from outside, causing the beast to momentarily shift its focus. I seized this precious distraction. Mustering every shred of my being, I allowed the zombie in me to take over, temporarily leaving my humanity behind. I launched myself towards the beast with a primal snarl.

I took savage blows, pain exploding across my form, yet I withstood it all. I realized the truth of a rather grim, yet literal truth - a zombie can survive anything as long as he keeps his head. My survival instincts, fueled by the unforgiving ferocity of my zombie nature, had never felt more alive.

Reaching for one of the sharp rods of iron from my makeshift splint, I plunged it into the beast's side. It let out a furious roar, but I was relentless, slashing open a large, gaping wound. With a gritted snarl, I rammed my infected arm deep into the wound, our bloods mingling. For a split second, we were one, understanding each other's essence. As my blood mixed with the beast's, our identities blurred together, each of us feeling the other's essence. I saw a monstrous creature that was a reflection of my own desperate fight for survival, its anger and hunger mirroring my worst fears. My heart pounded in sync with its pulse, thumping against my ribcage like a war drum.

"I can save you," I pleaded, my voice echoing through the cavern. The transformation into a full zombie was pulling at every fiber of my being, pain throbbing from every wound. But I wasn't about to let that extinguish the spark of hope in my eyes.

The beast's laugh was a disturbing rumble that vibrated in the air between us. It spat out words soaked in venom, "Save me? There's nothing to save, Lance. I was always a monster. Just like you."

"No!" I shouted back, denying his claim with every ounce of my being. "We're not monsters. We're victims. Victims of a world that has turned its back on us. But it's not too late for you."

An eerie silence filled the cavern, charged with tension and mutual understanding. Then, the beast roared, lunging towards me with claws extended towards my throat.

In that instant, I knew I had no choice. The man had chosen his fate, willingly embracing his monstrous form. Yet, I felt a pang of regret for what could have been, for the lives we might have saved together.

My blood, coursing through its veins, started to reverse the beast's transformation. It was just enough. Summoning all my strength, I ripped into its back, my hands closing around its backbone. His eyes flared in rage. I closed my eyes, refusing to witness the death of a monster that was, in many ways, just like me. With a final cry, I tore the beast's spine from its body, the lifeless form crumpling to the ground with a sickening thud. Its terror-filled eyes stared blankly into the darkness, the once formidable beast reduced to a lifeless husk. My heart was heavy with the cost of our victory, a weight I knew I'd carry for the rest of my life.

It was over. Finally, it was over.

DAY ONE, YEAR ZERO.

We emerged from the cavernous bowels of the military base, battered and bruised, yet alive. We were survivors, wearied from battle, but our spirits were unbroken. Silence cradled Harmony in her arms, their bond stronger than ever. Rain and her growing pups walked alongside, while Thunder, majestic as ever, carried the loss of Whisky with a somber dignity.

The world was still a desolate place, scarred by the undead and the terrible toll of war. Yet, with the dawn breaking over the horizon, it seemed a little less bleak. The world was not ending; it was simply starting anew, healing itself slowly but surely.

We knew that our journey was far from over. The challenge of survival had been met and overcome. But now, we faced a different battle - the battle of living, of rebuilding, of making a place for ourselves in this brave new world.

The path before us was uncharted, fraught with unseen dangers and countless trials. But we walked it together, under the first rays of the new dawn, our hearts filled with a quiet determination. The horrors of the past were behind us, and ahead lay the promise of a future - one we would carve out with our own hands, our own will.

As we moved forward, I took one last look at the crumbled fortress that had been the symbol of our oppression. It was a ruin now, a testament to our victory. The dawn cast long shadows behind us, promising a brighter tomorrow.

And so, we walked on, into the dawn of a new day, ready to face whatever this reborn world had in store for us. We had survived. Now, it was time to live.

Made in the USA
Middletown, DE
27 September 2023

39553823R00191